JOURNEY THROUGH *the* VALLEY

One Man's Story of Learning to
Trust Jesus with Work, Faith, and Family

DAVID BRENNER

Copyright © 2026 by David Brenner.

All rights reserved. No part of this publication may be reproduced, distributed, or transmitted in any form or by any means, including photocopying, recording or other electronic or mechanical methods without the prior written permission of the publisher, except in the case of brief quotations embodied in critical reviews and certain other noncommercial uses permitted by copyright law. For permission requests, write to the publisher at: info@bublish.com

Disclaimer

This memoir is an account of my personal experiences to the best of my recollection. However, in order to protect the privacy of the individuals involved, certain names, dates, locations, and identifying details have been changed.

The intention of this work is to convey the emotional and experiential reality of the events described, rather than a precise historical record. Any modifications were made solely to preserve the integrity of the story while honoring the confidentiality of those involved.

All Scripture quoted is taken from the Holy Bible, New International Version®, NIV®. Copyright ©1973, 1978, 1984, 2011 by Biblica, Inc.™ Used by permission. All rights reserved worldwide.

Editing, design, and distribution by Bublish

ISBN: 978-1-64704-994-2 (Paperback)
ISBN: 978-1-64704-995-9 (Hardcover)
ISBN: 978-1-64704-993-5 (eBook)
ISBN: 978-1-64704-996-6 (Audiobook)

First Printing edition 2025.

CONTENTS

Author's Note *v*

Chapter 1: Brothers In Arms *1*

Chapter 2: Falling For The American Dream *7*

Chapter 3: Growing Faith And Family *17*

Chapter 4: Embracing Life's Challenges *25*

Chapter 5: Learning To Trust Without Shame *35*

Chapter 6: Buckling Under Pressure *45*

Chapter 7: God Loves Me, Even At My Worst! *55*

Chapter 8: Two Competing Truths *63*

Chapter 9: Giving And Growing In Faith *71*

Chapter 10: Learning To Open My Hands *81*

Chapter 11: Breaking In The Tension *85*

Chapter 12: Hearing From Jesus *91*

Chapter 13: Learning Humility And Rest *99*

Chapter 14: Experiencing The Living God *107*

Chapter 15: Hearing From The Holy Spirit   *111*

Chapter 16: When The Holy Spirit Leads   *123*

Chapter 17: A Shift Of The Heart   *137*

Chapter 18: How Are You Not Okay?   *147*

Chapter 19: The Dark Night Of The Soul   *155*

Chapter 20: Hiking The Summit   *167*

Chapter 21: Finding Peace   *177*

Acknowledgements   *185*

Author Bio   *187*

AUTHOR'S NOTE

I am an unlikely author for a book on faith. I'm not a pastor or theologian. And despite being raised in the church, I spent many years viewing faith as a checklist of dos and don'ts. I thought I could live life *my* way and still be a good Christian. I wanted to enjoy everything the world had to offer and do just enough in my faith to make it into heaven. I had no idea that as I climbed the corporate ladder at lightning speed, I was actually racing straight toward an iceberg.

By the time I was in my early thirties, I was a thriving executive and had a beautiful wife and growing family. Outside, it looked like the American dream. But inside, I was broken and falling apart. I'd stuffed down a mountain of hurt from my childhood and left Jesus on the sidelines. I felt unworthy and unloved. My pain expressed itself as anxiety, detachment, and anger. Despite all I'd achieved professionally, I didn't like the person I was becoming. Something had to change.

As the complexity of being an executive, husband, and father took hold of me, I began to look to Jesus to help me navigate the challenges of my journey. I began to exchange our culture's coping mechanisms for the spiritual practices that we see depicted throughout Scripture. I started reading the Bible consistently, poured out my hurt to Jesus in a journal, prayed, and attended a Christian men's group. These habits became a lifeline for me. Ever so slowly, I began to change as a man.

It was in the darkest of my valleys that I begged Jesus to take away my pain. But over time, I learned that these valleys weren't punishment but places of sacred trust where I was refined and finally able to surrender my way and my pain to Jesus. I became stronger each time I journeyed through a new valley. I found that it was actually in the silence where Jesus was at work in my life. He wanted me to understand that pain wasn't the enemy—it was the teacher. What I thought was a curse was actually a blessing.

I decided to share *Journey Through the Valley* because I want you know that you're not alone. My journey and growth as a disciple of Jesus has not been linear. And there were seasons where it felt like I was going backward despite fighting to walk forward. It has been more of a two-steps-forward, three-steps-back kind of trek. But I've discovered that in the valleys—where maximum effort feels like it yields only inches of progress—is where you plant the seeds of faith that have the potential to grow the most in years to come. Over time, the inches add up to miles. And while there's still a long road ahead, I no longer see the valley as a place to be feared.

It is my sincere hope that *Journey Through the Valley* will inspire you to trust the faithfulness of Jesus even in the darkest and most hopeless moments. No matter who you are, or what you've done, Jesus extends the same invitation to each one of us: "It's just a little bit further, you can do it. Get back up." Where the world offers striving and competition, Jesus offers peace. His offer is simple: "Take my yoke upon you and learn from me, for I am gentle and humble in heart, and you will find rest for your souls."

—David

Chapter 1

BROTHERS IN ARMS

Have you ever watched someone's world fall apart? I have, and it changed my life. Back in 2016, I was asked to join a men's spiritual leadership group. I still remember the invite for these 6:30 a.m. Saturday morning gatherings at one of our local breakfast restaurants only a few miles from my house. I thought my pastor was crazy—six thirty in the morning on a Saturday? After some personal reflection, I joined reluctantly. Right away it became clear these men were all on similar journeys, all trying to integrate faith, work, and family—just like I was. I'd never been part of a group like this before and after just one meeting, it became a vital part of my routine.

Over time we became close as we shared our challenges, successes, and failures at work and home—and our faith journeys. But something seemed off as I walked into our local breakfast restaurant on a particularly cold February morning. I grabbed my staple sausage, egg, and cheese on an everything bagel along with a large hazelnut coffee and headed over to the group. Everyone was there, but as we shared our weekly updates, I noticed Mark looking around the table with an unusual heaviness. When it was Mark's turn, his voice cracked as he spoke.

"It was a difficult week for me, guys. My house in Tennessee burned down."

There was a collective gasp and murmurs of condolence. Ray, a lawyer, asked what we were all wondering. "What happened, Mark?"

"Well, the fire marshal said the fireplace damper wasn't open and some stuff nearby the fireplace caught fire. He suspects the tenant either wasn't paying attention or wasn't close to the fireplace when sparks started to fly."

Everyone sat quietly, processing the gravity of Mark's crisis. We all knew this was a crippling blow to his finances. He was in his mid-sixties and had spent his whole life as a pastor. Our church was small and Mark worked a second job so as not to put additional financial strain on our small church. The rent from his previous home in Tennessee had provided his family with much-needed income.

"Was everything destroyed?" Ray followed up.

"Yes, a total loss. The house and everything in it is gone."

Max, a teacher who'd recently joined the group, asked. "Did everyone make it out okay?"

"Fortunately, no one was hurt," Pastor Mark replied with a sad smile.

It sounded like tenant negligence to me, so I chimed in with the next question. "Have you heard anything from your insurance company?"

And that's when the bottom fell out.

"Well, I just found out that my tenant is suing me for a million dollars. He's trying to say the fire was my fault."

None of us could believe what we were hearing. It didn't make sense and could mean financial ruin for our beloved pastor. I was sure I wasn't the only person in the room thinking, *How could God let this happen to such a faithful servant, to a man so devoted to Him?*

Humbled and broken, our pastor didn't have any answers that Saturday morning. What he did have was unwavering faith. From where all of us were sitting, it seemed as if his life had fallen apart. We couldn't believe how he was able to acknowledge the pain in his heart and still trust in God. Meanwhile the rest of us were trying to control our emotions. It was like we had witnessed the first punch in an unexpected fist fight. Pastor Mark tried to calm us all down.

> **Two things can be true at once. You can hurt and also trust Jesus amid the pain.**

"I really appreciate your concern," he said, resting his hands on the table, "but for me, I know that I just need to keep walking with Jesus and share with you how I do it. Every day we have a choice. No matter what the world throws at us, we still get to choose the lens we use to process it. We can use all our energy to fight back—like much of the world does—or we can use our energy to trust God and His Word. Each day we get to choose whether we'll believe His Word or follow the way of the world. That is the challenge—especially when the going gets tough."

I didn't realize it at the time but Pastor Mark was talking to us about spiritual formation, the process of becoming either more like Jesus or less like Him. C. S. Lewis said it like this:

> Every time you make a choice you are turning the central part of you, the part of you that chooses, into something a little different than it was before. You are slowly turning this central thing into a heavenly creature or a hellish creature: either into a creature that is in harmony with God, and with other creatures, and with itself, or else into one that is in a state of war and hatred with God, and with its fellow creatures, and with itself.[1]

What Pastor Mark was opening our eyes to that morning was that even when an event is unfair, unjust, or harmful to us, we still have a choice. We can trust God and lean on Him—or we can punch back. For a guy like me in his early thirties, this message of surrender was counter to everything I had witnessed in the world. It was hard to wrap my head around Pastor Mark's approach and even harder to put into practice. I had never seen anyone model this type of faith before. I also wasn't sure this type of faith applied to me as an emerging executive. It seemed as if he was asking us to embrace failure and tragedy. I had built my career anticipating problems and carrying my team to the finish line, regardless of the cost. Failure was never an option. Pastor Mark's approach sounded too passive to work for my proactive, type A personality. Yet there was something about his sense of genuine peace amid a major life crisis that caught my attention. This was a peace I did not have or understand.

As I got in my car and pulled away from the restaurant, my mind was racing. *How was this man so comfortable with vulnerability?* I wondered. I'd never seen a pastor reveal the challenges of following Jesus. And I'd certainly never had a front row seat to seeing a

---

1   The Great Divorce by C.S. Lewis published 1945

man's faith tested like this. I drove home in silence, feeling terrible for my pastor and grateful it wasn't me. I began to wonder, *Is Mark's crisis some kind of punishment from a harsh and distant God?* But it was the following thought that shook me to my core: *If this can happen to such a good and faithful man, what hope is there for an imperfect person like me?*

It would take a couple of years, but in the end, the tenant's court case against Pastor Mark would be dismissed and insurance would pay to restore his house in Tennessee. Mark and his family would come through a tough financial situation and those around our pastor would bear witness to his unwavering faith. But none of us knew any of this back on that cold Saturday morning in 2016. All we knew was that this man's world fell apart, and he was still able to express both deep anguish and trust in God. We were privileged to experience Pastor Mark's living master class on faith. It was a lesson none of us would ever forget—and all of us would soon desperately need. You see, one by one, over the course of the coming year, each of our worlds would begin to fall apart. Mine would be next. But unlike Pastor Mark, whose crisis was thrust upon him, my crisis had been slowly forming over the last decade. I had relentlessly pursued the American dream at all costs while ignoring Jesus's call to truly follow Him. I was so caught up in chasing success at all costs that I didn't realize I had sidelined my faith and my God—and I was blind to the warning signs that told me things were going to fall apart.

Chapter 2

FALLING FOR THE AMERICAN DREAM

I grew up in an upper middle-class home. My mom was a first-generation Christian who started following Jesus in high school and my dad started his faith journey a bit later, accepting Jesus's free gift of salvation shortly after he married my mom. By the time I was in elementary school, my parents were very involved in our local church and our family attended services almost every Sunday.

As a successful executive, my dad's career advancements moved us to six different states throughout my childhood. Like many, he struggled to balance the demands of his job with the calling of his faith and family. As his son, I had my own struggles. When I was just one year old, my mom found me struggling to breathe and rushed me to the hospital. The hospital put me in an oxygen tent, and my mom curled up next to me praying throughout the night that my life would be spared. I made it through but was diagnosed with severe asthma. The lack of oxygen to my brain resulted in me developing a debilitating learning disability called dysnomia. By the time I was five, my kindergarten teacher told my mom I'd never graduate from high school. In a beautiful expression of faith, my mom listened to what the teacher told her but rejected the teacher's prognosis. From speech therapists to a school for children with learning disabilities to spending every summer working on my writing skills, my mom fought for me with everything she had. With time, I was able to overcome my learning disability. Despite my academic improvement, though, I spent third through eighth grade being relentlessly picked on at school. While I'd overcome my learning disability, I hadn't figured out how to overcome my social awkwardness.

It was the '90s, and it seemed like every movie I watched was about a rich and successful young executive living the good life that dovetailed perfectly with the American dream. It was the life my dad was living, and it was exactly the life I wanted. It would take me years to realize that relentlessly pursuing the next accomplishment at all costs was a coping mechanism for me to drown out the unresolved hurt in my heart.

By the time I was twenty-three, I was well on my way to living the dream. I was equal parts ambitious and focused. I had received my bachelor's degree in two and a half years and earned my MBA while working full-time at a leading medical device company. Eventually I joined a major federal consulting firm and moved to Baltimore, Maryland. With my career now on the perfect trajectory, I wanted to relax and have some fun. There was a lot of drinking and some major life mistakes. I was successful, charming, and accepted—it was everything I'd dreamed of. But no one tells you about the hangovers, the despair, and the price you pay for living a toxic lifestyle. After eighteen months of restraint-free living and two selfish, life-altering wake-up calls, I knew that something needed to change.

As I looked into the mirror, I asked myself: *Is this who you have become? Is this who you really are?* I knew this was not the man I was created to be. I aspired to be a better version of myself. In the aftermath of my toxic lifestyle in Baltimore, I started attending church regularly and reading the Bible. Though I still struggled to walk with purity in the years that followed, my days of living recklessly were over. While I made small steps in my faith, I fell back into my old pattern of chasing success, and I buried myself in work.

By twenty-five, I was moving up the corporate ladder at one of the nation's best consulting firms, and I was already eyeing my next promotion. I'd moved from Baltimore to the Washington, DC, area. I was living just steps away from the Iwo Jima national monument in Arlington, Virginia. I mistakenly thought that if I just tried harder, I'd be able to sin less. While my resolve was fierce at first, I lacked consistency with the spiritual practices that could have helped me understand the true power of prayer, reading the Scriptures, journaling, and solitude. Eventually, time gave way to compromise.

Throughout my early twenties, I failed to realize how strong the pull toward sin was in my life. While I was going through the spiritual motions, I didn't understand the difference between reading my Bible to be a "good" Christian and studying the Scriptures to live my life more like Jesus. It would take years for me to truly believe that the way of life described in the Scriptures was the *best* way to live. Ultimately I learned that every day, we have a choice—just like C. S. Lewis said. We can either tap into the power of His Word—by confessing our sins, abiding by Jesus's standards—or we can rationalize our sins and hide from the truth. By choosing the former, we invite the Holy Spirit to rebuild the broken places in our lives. But in my youthful ignorance, I chose the latter, rationalizing my lifestyle choices in DC because they were better than the ones I'd made earlier in Baltimore. It didn't take long before my faith once again slid to the back seat.

> **Each day we get to choose if we'll be a little bit more or less like Jesus.**

It was amid this tension between following the world and following Jesus that I met my future wife. It was Labor Day 2010. I went to a barbecue and met Caitlin, a DC local. As a 5'9" physician assistant with blonde hair and big brown eyes, she immediately had my attention. She was smart, driven, and athletic—way out of my league. But we hit it off because we were both into triathlons. A few weeks after the barbecue, we had our first date. As I made my way through the city to meet her for dinner, I inhaled the crisp fall air. It was delightful; the three-mile walk to the restaurant gave me some time to take stock of my life. Work was exceeding my wildest expectations, and I was finally making enough money to really build up my savings. I was also in the best shape of my life, and now I was going on a date with an intelligent, gorgeous young woman. I thought to myself: *Could life get any better?*

Of course I was only looking at my life through the lens of the world around me—the money I was making, the professional titles I'd earned, and what I was accomplishing to build my resume. It felt as if I'd finally summited the mountain after years of hard work. Yet I failed to look at who I was becoming. If I'd been honest with myself in that moment, I would have realized that I was becoming a little less like Jesus each day. I had unknowingly lived life through our culture's definition of success instead of following the way of Jesus.

By the time I arrived at North Side Social, a trendy wine bar with spectacular hors d'oeuvres, the sun was already setting. It was the perfect atmosphere for a first date. As I sat across from Caitlin, I put my best foot forward. She was articulate and a deep thinker. I tried my best to match her depth as we jumped from topic to topic. There was a definite chemistry, and we talked for hours. Emboldened by the wine, her infectious smile, and my top-of-the-world confidence, I blurted out, "So what are your expectations for this relationship?"

She didn't miss a beat. With a relaxing, disarming smile, she replied with a shrug. "Nothing really. Whatever happens, happens."

Surely this couldn't be true, I thought. I was intrigued because I'd never heard such a casual response before. "No expectations?" I continued. "Really? Everyone has at least some unwritten rules."

"David," she said, leaning forward and staring right into my eyes. "I know a lot of girls have been dreaming of their wedding day since they were playing with dolls—but that's not me. I'm just taking life one day at a time. I'm good with wherever that takes me."

Finally, I thought. *A woman who checks all the boxes—beautiful, independent, and low-maintenance. I'll definitely be able to climb the corporate ladder with her by my side.* It wouldn't be until we were married with our first child that I would realize that our early nonchalance toward our relationship came not from wholeness but rather from a deep place of unexamined hurt. During the entirety of our three-hour first date, I never uttered a single word about my faith or even asked her about hers.

Despite our intentions to take it slow, we were soon seeing each other almost every day, even though we were both busy with our own careers and lives. Caitlin was much more adventurous than me, and I was desperate to show her that I could match her level of spontaneity. By the time we met, she had already been skydiving—something I'd never even considered. So when she asked me to hike one of the hardest mountains in the Shenandoah National Forest just a few months after we started dating, I said yes without missing a beat. It was an exhausting nine-mile, out-and-back hike with two thousand feet of elevation in the first five miles. I wasn't a complete stranger to hiking and had periodically hiked a couple of hard trails, but my idea of having a good time was more about relaxing in luxury than roughing it in the woods. And yet every time we went somewhere new, Caitlin wanted to explore it, primarily on foot. In order to impress her, I started hiking more often and learned to love it. Being out in nature would later become an important spiritual practice for me.

Our independence and low-maintenance mindsets kept things safe and contained in the early days of our relationship. Caitlin had been raised in a home that didn't prioritize faith, and she didn't see faith as a central tenant of her beliefs. I was still trying to figure out what my faith meant to me. With the demands of my career, I never had enough time to really think deeply about this major issue that seemed to simmer beneath the surface. Without even realizing it, I chose not to rock the boat and sidelined my faith. In hindsight, we both kept our heart wounds beneath the surface. When she wanted to stay out late at the bars with her friends, I didn't give her a hard time. When I called to tell her I had to work late, she made other plans without a fuss. I thought our relationship was carefree and thriving, but as work continued to escalate for me, so did the stress. Eventually the balancing act became harder and harder. Then, one Friday afternoon, about eighteen months into our relationship, my boss called me in a panic.

"David, I just got a call from our main government client. You know change is hard for them and this is an enormous, transformative project. The team at their data center isn't following the process and everyone is fighting. It's complete pandemonium and they are livid. Could you drive out to their data center and get things back on track?"

"Sure, no problem!" I responded without hesitation, even though it was a ninety-minute drive and I had planned to spend the evening with Caitlin. "Give me about ten minutes, and I'll be on the road."

I left Caitlin a voice message saying I had to put out a fire at work and arrived at the data center in good time. As I drove in, I felt like Superman swooping in to save the day. By the time I'd made it through all the organization's rigorous security checks, it was already six thirty in the evening. The client was in the middle of a simulation using the new IT system, and the programs weren't talking to each other. The integrations were breaking and the staff wasn't paying close enough attention to important alerts from the system. It was complete chaos, just like my boss had described.

As I walked into the room, I immediately realized the gravity of the situation. Sitting around the table was a mix of the deputy director's leadership team as well as subject matter experts from every area of the business. This was an organization that disliked outsiders and was ruthless in spotting and punishing errors. I had once witnessed an entire meeting halted for a minor grammatical error on a slide. I was in over my head the moment I walked in the room. *What did you get yourself into?* I thought. *With all this infighting, they're going to suck you in and spit you right back out. There's no way you can handle this.*

As the fear of failure swept over me, my heart began to race and my palms started sweating. Blood rushed to my face. I was about to fail before I even tried. Just when it felt like all hope was lost, the word *pray* popped into my mind. There had been a handful of these types of moments in my life before, when things were collapsing, and I'd thrown up an SOS to God. *Dear God, please don't let me crash the car! Dear Lord, please don't let me get in trouble with my dad! Jesus, please help me out of this freezing water!* So I gave it a try. "Jesus," I whispered. "I am completely out of my depth. Please, could You help me? Give me wisdom to handle this chaos." In the moments that followed, my breathing calmed, my heart rate slowed, and I was able to find my words.

> **It doesn't matter how many times you've messed up; Jesus won't give up on you.**

With a touch of boyish charm, I asked the senior leaders where they were having the most trouble. Eventually I found myself at the desk of an expert who'd spent their thirty-year career focusing on the part of the system that was breaking. I moved from discussion to discussion, expert to expert. Whenever my heart began to race, I would whisper another quick prayer and lean into the moment. It felt like Jesus was extending His hand to me, whispering ever so softly, "Let me teach you a different way."

Taking charge and being proactive instead of reactive made all the difference. As late evening gave way to the wee hours of the morning, I could tell that something special had occurred over the six hours I was there. At three in the morning, I finally began my ninety-minute drive back home and fell into bed exhausted.

The next morning, my phone rang while I was still in bed.

"Good morning, David," my sleepy brain heard my boss say with unmistakable enthusiasm. "I spoke with the client. You did a stellar job. They've asked us to stand up a special support team for the go live, and I'd like you to be one of the leads."

I was thrilled and thanked God for guiding me through a tough situation. For the first time in my life, my faith and work began to merge. I was now on the leadership team of a critical project. Week after week, my short prayers during the day gave way to studying the Scriptures before and after work—and longer prayers in my more peaceful moments. As the project neared completion, I thought: *At every step, there have been countless land mines. Even some of my bosses have been tripped up and suffered the consequences. It has been months, but I haven't tripped a single land mine. How is that possible?* Then a new thought bubbled up in my mind: *These are lottery odds.* I'd never thought about faith being exciting. But bringing my faith into work felt so different from the rote, dry faith of my childhood. *This is fun,* I thought, *really fun. I like this faith adventure.* In the middle of this revelation, a prayer emerged: *Jesus, I have never had to depend on You like this in my life. Would You keep the challenges coming so I always have to depend on You?*

Ultimately, the project was a smashing success, and I was promoted to manager. I had taken my first

> **Jesus didn't come for us to follow an endless list of rules; He came so that we could experience the Kingdom of God. Here. Now.**

real steps as an adult in my faith, calling out to Jesus for help, and in the process I had picked up the scent of a different way of living. Still, there was a long road ahead. I had finally found the trailhead for my faith journey. Even though I had believed in Jesus for my whole life, I was essentially still an infant in my faith. The long journey ahead would be a three-steps-forward, two-steps-back experience, but I had finally begun in earnest.

Chapter 3

GROWING FAITH AND FAMILY

After several months in my coveted new position with the same client, I decided I wanted to take advantage of one of the position's perks: I could live in a different city and fly into DC each week to work. I was thrilled by the chance to be closer to my mom and dad, who now lived in Florida, but was nervous to broach the subject with Caitlin. We were getting more serious, and I was wrestling with conflicting feelings about my growing faith and Caitlin's close-mindedness about Jesus. In one of my more cowardly moments, I took my mom up on her offer to fly Caitlin down to Florida for a weekend to get to know her and talk about faith.

"How was the trip?" I asked when Caitlin arrived back from Florida late on a Sunday night.

Flustered and confused, she replied, "David, I just spent an entire weekend with your mother, and she told me how important your faith is to you. How come I am finding this out just now—and from your mother and not you?"

I fumbled for words. "It just seems like you're not really interested in spiritual things. You get really defensive and say religion isn't for you. I was just worried you wouldn't want to be with me if I told you about my faith."

Caitlin let out a sigh. "Well, at least now I know."

Finally mustering an ounce of courage, I continued. "I think if you're willing to come to church with me, Caitlin, you might just see that following Jesus is more than just a religious thing."

> **Faith isn't about perfection; it's about walking, stumbling, and getting back up.**

Caitlin had only been inside a church a few times in her entire life, so when she first joined me for a service on Sunday, her discomfort was palpable. When the offering basket came around in the middle of the service, I took out the check I'd written for $300 and dropped it in. Her eyes rolled, and her gasp was audible. Despite her reluctance, she kept coming with me each week. I appreciated how hard she was trying. But the tension in our relationship kept building as we both tried to figure out if we wanted to get married. In my nightly prayers, I rambled awkwardly before Jesus. "I don't understand how I can feel so strongly toward Caitlin with my heart but stay true to Scripture when Paul in 2 Corinthians says I shouldn't be 'unequally yoked with an unbeliever.'" This prayer marked the first time I really examined my life against the words of Scripture. It was in this moment of tension and confusion that I found my heart longing to invite Jesus into the moment.

By the time I had the firm's final approval to relocate, it was late in 2012, and I'd pushed off the conversation with Caitlin for far too long. So, on a cold Saturday afternoon, as we were walking from her townhouse to my car, a mere forty steps, I swung around and blurted out my decision to move to Florida, a decision I'd made without her.

Caitlin stopped in her tracks and stared at me in complete shock. "You're not even going to talk to me about this? You're moving to Florida? What about me?"

Somehow I hadn't even noticed the blow that I'd just dealt her, and I continued matter-of-factly. "I'll still be up here four days a week, so we can see each other then—or you can move down to Florida with me, if you want."

"I would *never* move somewhere for a *boyfriend*," she said emphatically.

"Yes, you've always said that," I responded calmly. "I know what it would take to bring you to Florida."

We had now been dating for two years. I had always thought that I'd know definitively if I was going to marry someone after dating for that long. But I was too focused on work. I didn't have time for the type of self-reflection necessary to make such a critical life choice. I also lacked the maturity and empathy to consider Caitlin's needs and perspective. And although I was praying and reading the Bible more, it was still a new habit. At the time, I thought the habit made me faithful. But I was not yet full of faith; I was only scratching the surface, still leading an unexamined life—and Caitlin was a victim of my lack of understanding. In the aftermath of our conversation, I could sense the distance between us growing. It was as if we both knew a breakup was on the horizon.

As I prepared for my move to Florida, the tension with Caitlin about our future led to a hunger and desire to pray. I was now spending time studying the Bible almost daily—and what I was reading was captivating my heart. I was beginning to see that our culture's definition of success was not the same as God's. As I read Galatians 5, Paul's words started to make more sense: "For the flesh desires what is contrary to the Spirit, and the Spirit what is contrary to the flesh. They are in conflict with each other, so that you are not to do whatever you want."

I even began to read the Bible in front of Caitlin—and something strange and wonderful happened. She began engaging more and asking me questions about my faith. It was clear she was re-evaluating her own strongly held beliefs about Jesus and His free gift of salvation. Then one day after work, out of the blue, she said, "I'm not going to give up on us. You're unlike anyone I've ever dated, and I see a future together."

Her words caught me off guard. Perhaps for the first time, I felt valued and seen by the woman I loved. I had seen her transformation as she slowly and cautiously opened her life to Jesus and started her own faith journey. Realizing how poorly equipped I was to make such a monumental decision, I fervently began to pray to Jesus for his approval or denial to marry Caitlin. I prayed about it throughout each week, but day after day my prayers were met with silence. I was determined and found myself remembering one of the parables Jesus told in Luke 11—the story of the persistent neighbor asking for bread and eventually receiving it: "So, I say to you: Ask and it will be given to you; seek and you will find; knock and the door will be opened to you. For everyone who asks receives; the one who seeks finds; and to the one who knocks, the door will be opened."

I kept asking, but the silence was deafening. Still, I was determined to hear from Jesus. I created a playlist of worship music and set aside the entire night to pray for clarity. As night turned into evening and evening turned into the early morning hours, I kept battling to stay awake as bouts of dozing off hit me wave after wave. Amid my tired eyes doing their best to stay awake, I sensed the gentleness of Jesus's presence and a whisper bubbling up from inside of me. Jesus had finally answered my question and said yes to our marriage.

In the weeks that followed, I bought an engagement ring and made plans to propose on April 1 in front of the US Capitol. That year, Easter fell on March 31, and as the pastor of our church in South Florida concluded his message, he reminded the congregation of the free gift of salvation that Jesus offers. Caitlin was in DC watching the service online and called after to tell me she'd prayed to accept Jesus. She told me she was finally realizing that throughout her life, Jesus had been pursuing her, protecting her, and calling her to Him. As she spoke, tears welled up in my eyes as I whispered to Jesus, *Only You could bring light into the darkness and create something out of nothing.* The best part was that Caitlin had no idea that I planned to propose to her the next day.

Six months later, in September 2013, we tied the knot just outside DC. Though wonderful, our wedding was a comedy of errors. Unbeknownst to us, the officiant was not licensed to marry us in the state of Virginia. Then one of my groomsmen passed out, and when I went to stomp on the glass to celebrate our union, it shot out of the casing and flew down the aisle. At the reception, our caterers cut up our large cake in the kitchen and only put out our tiny six-inch wedding cake in the

> **When we trust Jesus with our lives, nothing is wasted. He brings beauty out of the ashes.**

center of the reception. It was wildly embarrassing. But none of it mattered because we were surrounded by friends and family. We were on top of the world.

The next day we headed to the airport and began our honeymoon. For three weeks, we toured Italy, from the canals in Venice to the breathtaking seaside villages of Cinque Terre on the country's west coast. We were immersed in Italy's beauty, culture, food, and wine. For our last few days, we checked into the Waldorf Astoria just a few miles outside of Rome. The balcony of our junior suite looked out on the countryside from atop a large hill. We enjoyed the magnificent view while sipping fine wine and nibbling delicious chocolates—compliments of the hotel to congratulate us on our marriage. It was the type of honeymoon that dreams are made of. But, as had been the norm for the entirety of our relationship, we kept things light. We were on our honeymoon but failed to connect to the deepest places of our hearts. We failed to dream together. We were newlyweds who still didn't really know each other despite being together for three years. Sure, I knew Caitlin's likes and dislikes, but I didn't know what shaped her thoughts and behaviors. I didn't know what was in her heart. I had fallen for our culture's view of marriage, which is best summarized by the famous Tom Cruise line from *Jerry McGuire*, "You complete me." I had no idea that marriage required me to leave behind my independence and become one with my wife, as Matthew 19:4–5 says: "Have you not read that he who created them from the beginning made them male and female, and said, 'Therefore a man shall leave his father and his mother and hold fast to his wife, and the two shall become one flesh'?"

It was upon arriving home that we discovered our officiant's lack of credentials in Virginia. It would take another six months and a formal petition to the courts in Virginia for our marriage to finally be recognized in 2014. But by that time, we were both living full-time in Florida and planning to start our family. The excitement of traveling throughout Italy had quickly given way to the challenges of navigating our chaotic first year of marriage. Caitlin had never lived alone before, and I was still traveling four days a week from Florida back to DC. She was also working sixty-plus hours a week in a job that took everything out of her. It was amid my constant traveling and Caitlin's brutal work schedule that our missed expectations simmered below the surface and remained unspoken due to our inability to connect deeply as a couple. We were together, but separate. Married, but alone. We were fine with the "for better" part of our marriage vows but ill-equipped to navigate the "for worse" aspects of life. It wasn't a great feeling, and we were floundering. I'd spent my whole life preparing to be a successful executive but found myself wildly unprepared to be a good husband. *What did I get myself into?* I asked. *How could things go south so quickly?* As I became aware of my thoughts, I began to pray: *Jesus, how do I fix this? We're not even a year into our marriage and everything is breaking.*

Unable to confide in each other about the deep places of hurt and brokenness, we settled into a rhythm of physically living together while being emotionally apart. Each Thursday night when I'd return from DC, I'd walk into our apartment around ten in the evening, and a similar dialogue would occur. It was almost emotionless.

"How did your week go?" I'd ask.

Caitlin, with her head still buried in her computer working on her charts, would look up and say, "Fine."

"What are your plans for tomorrow?" I'd probe.

"Probably run and then go to work."

I tried harder. "Do you want to grab dinner after?"

"Sure, that sounds fine."

Off I'd go to unpack. Time and time again I was unable to find the right words to capture her heart. We were two ships passing in the night despite both of us trying to grow in our faith. The hurt and pain washed over me like waves wearing down a sandcastle. I felt hopeless. I struggled to understand how life was getting more difficult even as I was working harder to follow Jesus. I prayed: *Jesus, I thought getting married was supposed to make us better, but it seems like we're only getting worse. Would You help us? Would You help me?*

A few weeks later, Caitlin walked into our living room where I was reading the Scriptures. "What are you doing over there in the corner?" she asked offhandedly.

Caught off guard, I looked up from my Bible and blurted out, "I'm learning how to be a better husband for you." I'd said it almost by accident, but those words opened a door to Caitlin's heart.

In the weeks that followed, I started to see my wife's hidden pain in plain sight and recognize everything she'd left behind to marry me. She had moved from DC, where she'd spent the last thirty years of her life. She was living alone in a new state where she didn't know anyone while I was traveling for work four days each week. Her new job in Florida was demanding and stressful. All at once, I knew I had to find a way to stop traveling so I could be more present. But I was going to move heaven and earth to fix the problem. I requested a transfer to the firm's newest and local office so I wouldn't have to travel anymore.

> **Jesus is faithful, even in the heartache and confusion.**

Chapter 4

EMBRACING LIFE'S CHALLENGES

At the end of 2014, my transfer to our local office was finally approved. We'd held our marriage together through a tough first year, though neither Caitlin nor I had yet learned how to look beneath the surface and talk about what was going on in our hearts. As we settled in as first-time homeowners, we found a small church of only one hundred people. That's when we met Pastor Mark. It was unlike any church I'd attended growing up. We went from friendless in southern Florida to belonging to a tight-knit church community of young married couples. At a potluck a few weeks after joining, I looked around and thought, *I can't believe how all of this fell into place so quickly. I cried out and You answered!* I was home each night with my wife, we were making friends, and our marriage was starting to heal. Soon, we joined the ranks of expectant parents, learning that our first son was on the way. On a cool spring morning, I prayed. *Jesus, I'm so grateful for Your protection of our marriage and so hopeful for the future.*

Work was going well, too. I was playing to all my strengths and helping the new business unit thrive. And with no travel, I was finally enjoying a great work-life balance. But with a child on the way, it wasn't long until my mind began to drift toward the additional expenses a child would bring. This tiny spark was all I needed to reignite my quest to advance my career again. I remember being in the middle of a monthly leadership update and thinking, *Why are these people senior managers? Their presentation skills aren't any better than mine. They don't mentor their staff very well. They don't even know the facts of their projects that well.* Then, almost without thinking, I took my own bait. I began saying to myself: *I could do a better job than these guys. Why can't I be a senior manager?*

After dinner that evening, I shared my idea with Caitlin. "So I might be able to make senior manager this year, if I push hard at work."

"Are you sure that's a good idea?"

"Yeah, I mean it's a long shot for me to even be considered, but I feel like I'm already starting to perform at the next level, so it shouldn't be too much more work."

Perplexed, Caitlin responded, "I still don't think it's a good idea with the baby coming. But I won't stop you if that's what you think is best."

As the conversation came to a close, I felt exhilarated by the chance of getting promoted. Meanwhile, Caitlin's hesitation barely registered as a concern. I told myself I was pursuing a promotion to support the needs of my growing family. In reality, I was once again bowing to the pressure of our "success at all costs" culture, which was drowning out the words of Jesus, who was trying to help me understand the true desires of my heart. A few days later,

I found a free moment in my boss's schedule and knocked on his door. "Got a second?" I asked casually.

He closed his laptop and gave me his full attention. "Sure, David, what's on your mind?"

"I was hoping we could talk about my career. I feel like I've been adding real value to the business and wanted to understand what you'd need to see from me to make senior manager."

"David, as you know, the senior manager title comes with even greater responsibilities for billable hours, proposal wins, and revenue generation. You would have to go back into client services and pick up some projects to make a case for that promotion."

But I'm crushing it, I thought. *How could I have to prove myself even more?* Without weighing the full gravity of my director's very deliberate statement, I barreled ahead, dead set on proving myself.

"I understand. But if I were able to build up a portfolio of successful projects on top of my current job responsibilities, would I have your support?"

He paused and reflected thoughtfully. I was sure he was considering my young age. I was only thirty.

"Yes, David, if your portfolio is successful, I think you could be ready to present your value proposition during the year-end review process."

> **Chasing after success will leave you empty; it's like chasing after a vapor.**

And there it was, the phrase I'd been waiting to hear—the value proposition, a ten-minute rite-of-passage pitch to the partners of the firm. Those invited would create a slide presentation and make the case as to why *they* should be promoted to senior manager. If I could just get an invite, I knew I'd have a shot.

As our meeting came to a close, I began to daydream. *I could be a senior manager by the end of the year!* Without even realizing it, I'd subconsciously made a choice that put at risk everything bringing me peace and joy. I thought my heart was in the right place, but I hadn't studied the Scriptures deeply enough to be aware of the words David writes in Psalm 139:23–24: "Search me, God, and know my heart; test me and know my anxious thoughts. See if there is any offensive way in me and lead me in the way everlasting."

In a flash, I was off to find the key projects I needed to secure my pitch opportunity. These projects would be added to my current workload, so I had to choose wisely. I met with every director and senior manager I knew. I explained what I was trying to achieve and asked them to help me find the right projects. The first project came from my previous work with my old government client from DC. *Perfect!* I thought. I knew how their organization operated. I knew their vernacular, their work culture, and what success looked like to them. It seemed simple and straightforward. From what I'd heard, the project was going smoothly, so all I needed to do was make sure everything stayed on track. This would take maybe five hours of extra work per week. Given that I was only working forty hours a week at this time, this seemed very manageable.

Within a few weeks of taking on the new project, Caitlin was scheduled to be induced at a nearby hospital that we jokingly called the Waldorf Astoria because it was so high-end. In the last few weeks of Caitlin's pregnancy, our son's growth had begun to slow, so out of an abundance of caution, the doctor had decided to induce at forty weeks. Our son would be named Joshua. Caitlin was gracious in allowing our son to be named after the great Jewish leader who led the Israelites into the promised land.

As we pulled into the parking lot, I grabbed Caitlin's hand, and we prayed together. "Jesus, thank You for guiding us through these last nine months. We're so excited to meet Joshua. Please give Caitlin strength for the challenges that lie ahead. I ask You to protect both her and Joshua as he begins the process to enter our world. Amen." We took pictures on our phones as we entered the hospital, both excited and proud. *Everything is perfect*, I thought.

The check-in process was seamless and within an hour Caitlin was in the labor and delivery room receiving Pitocin to induce Joshua's birth. But after a few hours of contractions, the Doctor walked in looking worried. "Caitlin, your labor is not progressing the way we'd hoped. I'm noticing some pretty concerning deceleration in your baby's heart rate." I held Caitlin's hand as the Doctor continued. "I am going to move you to a C-section."

I felt helpless as I watched devastation creep across Caitlin's face. She had done everything right during her pregnancy. She was in fantastic shape. She ate well. She got plenty of sleep. We had prayed together throughout her pregnancy. But despite all this, everything was going wrong. *Why is this happening to us, God?*

I began texting our close friends, asking them to pray for Caitlin and Joshua. I closed my eyes and prayed, too. *Jesus, I know You are with us, but we are scared. Please protect Caitlin and give our doctor the skill and insight to bring Joshua into this world.*

Caitlin was quickly prepared for surgery and was soon lying on the operating room table. As I sat holding my wife's hand, I could see her body starting to shake against the table as the cold temperature of the operating room combined with the side effect of the numbing medication for her C-section. I whispered, "You're doing great. I know you're cold, but the doctor is almost done. Just a little bit more to go." I tried to sound calm for my wife, but in my head, I kept praying. *Father, please protect them. Please bring my wife and son through this.*

Time stood still as the doctor worked to bring Joshua into this world. At each step along the way, our doctor gave us calm, brief updates. Finally, we heard the beautiful cry of our son Joshua. He was alive! I watched as the doctor handed our tiny baby to the nurses to clean him up. But my heart immediately sank, as my eyes struggled to adjust to what I was seeing. Joshua was a deep shade of purple. Even to me, it was clear he was not getting enough oxygen. *Please, don't take him from us!* I shouted silently. *Please, have mercy on my innocent boy!* The nurses moved with mastery to clear Joshua's tiny passageways and within a minute, his body started to turn from purple to peach. I let out a grateful gasp. "Thank You, Jesus!"

Unaware of what I had just witnessed, Caitlin asked to see Joshua. Within a few moments, the nurses placed our tiny, six-pound-five-ounce newborn on his mother's chest. Despite the somewhat chaotic and sterile setting, it was a moment when heaven touched earth. As I awkwardly cradled Caitlin's head in my arm and placed my hand over our tiny son, I was immersed in the beauty of family. I thought to myself, *Today your whole body fits in my hand, Joshua. But one day you'll be taller than me. You are such a gift.*

In the weeks that followed, Joshua struggled to eat and sleep but made a full recovery from his traumatic delivery. Caitlin's recovery would be slower. I had eight weeks of paternity leave to help out after her maternity leave ended. But I questioned my abilities as a father. My brain was filled with self-doubt. *You're not made for this, David. You don't know how to do this. You're going to fail.* I had spent all my energy trying to improve my professional skills but had never prepared myself to be a good husband or father. I was in desperate need of help, yet I didn't yet understand how to pray to Jesus in these smaller everyday moments.

It was in this state of anxiety and searching that I began attending Pastor Mark's men's group, which was a breath of fresh air. Each week my eyes were being opened to a different way of thinking about following Jesus and my faith. *I can't believe how incredible each of the men in this group are,* I thought. *Their encouragement helps me continue on when I want to run away from work. And Pastor Mark's guidance feels like he's repouring my spiritual foundation.*

I had spent the last few years trying to walk out my journey of faith in the dark and alone. Now, as part of Pastor Mark's group, I felt for the first time that the lights were finally on. I was inspired by Mark's vulnerability and transparency in how he lived out his faith, even in times of crisis. Each week he passionately pleaded with us to create a rhythm of life where we could make time to process our thoughts and feelings before Jesus.

> **Our faith is strongest when we do life with others and don't hide from our hurt.**

As he showed us his journal, I chuckled. *I thought only women journaled.* But I respected this man, so I decided to give it a shot. Stopping on the way home from one of our meetings, I walked into our local Walmart. Amid the many pink, floral, and pastel journals, I eventually found a simple brown hardcover journal with the word notes printed on the front. That evening, I made my first entry:

Jesus,

This 192-page journal is twice the size I had in mind. I think what You're telling me is that I won't write a page a day but that I should write what I can and to not be so task-oriented. I am so grateful for Your provision to give me these eight weeks off for paternity leave to seek You. I feel in just this week You are healing years of damage. I am so scared and excited. So, as I step out further into the water, I want to thank You for the community You've blessed me with—how You've brought these men of God into my life and delivered me in my work.

I would go on to write about all the unknowns that were creating fear in my heart. Each time I journaled, I would release all the pressures bottled up deep inside me. Journaling quickly became an important part of my weekly rhythm. Thankfully, this new practice came into my life at just the right time.

> **Journaling is one of the best tools we have for excavating our heart and finding what's beneath the surface.**

Before I knew it, my paternity leave was over and I was back at work. I had asked for new projects to show the firm that I was ready to be a senior manager, and now, just as I was in the midst of figuring out fatherhood, my new project at work began to veer offtrack. Though the problem wasn't of my creation, it was now my headache. Our developers were new to the firm and they were used to a much slower pace of work. They were missing milestones and failing the firm's quality reviews. I wasn't a developer, so I couldn't step in and fix the broken code; I could only try to manage the chaos. This meant extra hours and more stress than I'd initially thought I'd have to handle. The timing could not have been worse for my family.

As my problems at work continued to mount, the stress at home increased, too. For the first time, I did something radically different with my stress—I poured out my hurt into the pages of my journal. Each time life didn't go my way, my faith was turned upside down. I'd cry out silently from the depths of my heart, *God, why are You allowing this to happen? The harder I try to follow You, the tougher my life gets! I don't understand.* In my mind, I was doing the work—providing for my family, journaling, going to Pastor Mark's Christian men's group, and studying the Bible. But instead of being rewarded, I felt like God wasn't showing up. To me, it seemed like a simple equation—one plus one should equal two. But I only understood our world's definition of success. Despite having read the entire Bible, I still failed to understand that God's kingdom is different than the world. In His kingdom, hardship refines us and makes us stronger. It is a gift. James, the half-brother of Jesus, wrote about this in James 1:2–3: "Consider it pure joy, my brothers and sisters, whenever you face trials of many kinds, because you know that the testing of your faith produces perseverance."

I found myself torn. I wanted the good life I'd seen in the movies and thought Jesus would provide it if I just worked and prayed hard. Yet the more I followed Jesus, the more He asked me to trust that life's challenges had a purpose. He wanted me to do the work while I just wanted him to take away the burden. My faith was growing, but I was asking Jesus to show up like a genie and perform miracles.

> **Jesus uses the hard places in our life to transform us; pain isn't the problem—it's the fuel.**

When He didn't, I doubted His love for me. It would be years before I understood the message spoken of in Isaiah 55:8–9: "'For my thoughts are not your thoughts, neither are your ways my ways,' declares the Lord. 'As the heavens are higher than the earth, so are my ways higher than your ways and my thoughts than your thoughts.'" I understood these words on the surface but wasn't yet capable of embracing their true meaning in my heart. I was still trying to be the king of my world instead of surrendering to His will. However, it was these struggles that compelled me to stick to journaling each night, which was creating a daily practice that was slowly rewiring my thinking and redirecting my heart. I sat down at my desk, awkwardly trying to get my thoughts out onto the paper.

> Jesus,
>
> This week broke me to my core. I don't have the strength, desire, or energy to continue at work. If this is really where You want me, would You give me the fortitude I need and the perspective that I'm missing? I feel like I'm fiercely going after You, but You're only filling me up halfway. I'm confused and I really don't know how to continue.

I was upset that Jesus was no longer delivering the life, liberty, and pursuit of happiness that I wanted on a silver platter. I'd always been able to measure my progress on the road to success. From grades and advancing through school each year to climbing the corporate ladder, I could always see exactly where I was and define a clear next step. But what I was experiencing now seemed like a journey without a road map.

Chapter 5

LEARNING TO TRUST WITHOUT SHAME

Despite my continuing doubts about God's love for me, I kept attending the men's group where I continued to watch Pastor Mark live a faith-filled life, even amid major life challenges. There was such a stark difference between how I questioned God about everything and how Pastor Mark was being drawn closer to Jesus through his suffering. I was facing foothills and doubting God while he was climbing mountains and trusting God. Finally, at one of our early Saturday morning gatherings, I found the courage to open up to everyone.

"These last couple weeks," I shared, "I feel like I've been wearing my shoes on the wrong feet. I just keep getting tripped up at every turn. Work is a complete mess, and I can't seem to find the right words when I talk to Caitlin. We're not doing well, and I never knew that being a dad would be this hard."

"We all go through lulls in our career and challenges at home," Ray chimed in. "You'll be okay. Don't worry, David, you've got this."

Feeling like he didn't really understand the stakes, I clarified how bad work was going. "Thanks, Ray. I get that, but this project I'm working on to get promoted feels like it could catch on fire at any moment. I'm using every tool I've learned but I'm barely keeping it together. If this project goes down, my chances of promotion are done—maybe forever."

"So where do you see Jesus moving in this moment?" Pastor Mark asked.

His gentle question hit a nerve I didn't even know was there. I nodded quietly, but inside I silently cried out, *He's not!*

"David," Pastor Mark continued, "I bet if you spent some time with Jesus, processing your fear and hurt, you might find that He is present with you in this exact moment—even in your pain and His silence."

Pastor Mark's message hit differently that morning because this wasn't advice from someone whose life was a walk in the park. He was in the thick of the worst life could throw at a person. He had told us about his house in Tennessee burning down and being sued just a week earlier. Yet there he was in front of us still finding the courage to trust in God. I understood what he was saying but I was still struggling to integrate this level of faith into my daily life.

As the group came to a close, Pastor Mark's words echoed in my head. *Where do you see Jesus moving in this moment?* I felt that I was genuinely doing my part, but I couldn't understand why everything was getting worse. "How could You bring me this far,

God, only to abandon me?" I wrote in my journal that night. I was terrified of failing and that fear drove me to hurl accusations against God's deafening silence. I realized that a deeper question was emerging from the depth of my heart. Did I really trust Jesus? I was beginning to realize that I trusted Jesus with my eternity but not with my tomorrow. My head began to swirl as I thought: *Would a good God let Mark's house burn and someone sue him?* He was literally a pastor—a man of God—and one of the best people I'd ever met. *How can I trust a God that lets things like that happen to good people?* It would take me years to realize that Jesus actually addressed this issue head on when He said in John 16:33: "I have told you these things, so that in me you may have peace. In this world you will have trouble. But take heart! I have overcome the world."

Later that night, my mind drifted back to the Bible stories I'd read growing up. How could I trust a God who allowed the Israelites to be conquered and enslaved? Without realizing it, I was putting God on trial—and He wasn't defending himself against my accusations. In what felt like a never-ending silence, I was reminded of another time when God didn't respond to harsh accusations. It was when Jesus was at his trial before Pontius Pilate in Matthew 27. The thought sent shivers through my whole body. After over a decade of trying to be the king of my own life, I was finally beginning to see that I hadn't allowed Jesus to be King over my life.

Like a skydiver taking his first jump, I wondered, *Will the parachute really open?*

What if You tell me to walk away from my job and become a missionary in Africa? I worried that trusting God would compel me to live a life of poverty. I knew that His ways were very different than my ways or what I'd learned from the world. Despite knowing this truth deep in my bones, I struggled to trust Him with everything. And yet, it was in this struggle that my faith was being stretched and growing.

To answer my growing list of questions, I turned to the Bible. *I'll re-read the story of the Israelites to see what the prophets said on God's behalf,* I told myself. *I'm going to let God's Word speak for itself and figure out for myself if I can trust God.*

At the end of each long day, after everyone was asleep, I opened my Bible to see where God was in the story of the Israelites. I started with the Book of Joshua. On three separate occasions, God encourages Joshua to be strong and courageous as he leads the Israelites into the promised land. But when I reached Joshua 7, a light bulb went off. After an epic victory, when the Israelites brought down the walls of Jericho, they then proceeded to a town called Ai. It was so small they didn't even bother to bring the whole army. They sent only three thousand soldiers and the Israelites were overwhelmingly defeated. Despite knowing this Bible story, I'd somehow never really paid close attention to what was recorded in Joshua 7:7:

> And Joshua said, "Alas, Sovereign Lord, why did you ever bring this people across the Jordan to deliver us into the hands of the Amorites to destroy us? If only we had been content to stay on the other side of the Jordan!"

As I sat on the couch, my heart leaped out of my chest. *That's exactly how I've been feeling! Why bring me this far just to abandon me?* Like Joshua, I felt that at the first sign of failure, God had abandoned me. Like Joshua, I struggled to understand and trust God's infinite power. Paul says it like this in Romans 8:28: "And we know that God causes everything to work together for the good of those who love God and are called according to his purpose for them."

The story didn't end there for Joshua. He learned from God that they were defeated because someone named Aachen had sinned. After dealing with the sin, God told Joshua the strategy for victory: attack and retreat again—only this time, set up an ambush when you retreat. The people of Ai, confident after their first victory, charged the Israelites and walked right into Joshua's ambush. With God's help, the Israelites' initial humiliation became their strategy for victory. Ai's army was completely destroyed, their king was killed, and the city was reduced to a heap of rubble.

Like Joshua, I had struggled to be courageous and completely trust God. Hebrews 11:33–34 captures perfectly God's unmatched ability to turn even the worst of circumstances into victory:

> Who through faith conquered kingdoms, administered justice, and gained what was promised; who shut the mouths of lions, quenched the fury of the flames, and escaped the edge of the sword; whose weakness was turned to strength; and who became powerful in battle and routed foreign armies.

The story of the Israelites' victory in Ai gave me hope that my mistakes and weaknesses weren't the end of my story. *God is more powerful and faithful than I'd ever imagined,* I thought, with a great sense of relief.

Next, I read through the Book of Judges, highlighting the leaders who governed over Israel. Those who grew up in church probably remember that Samson was a judge who accomplished mighty things, but what I didn't notice was the Israelites' pattern of walking away from God. For hundreds of years, the Israelites were in a pattern of turning away from God, only to be brutally oppressed by an enemy. From there the Israelites would cry out to God, and God would bring a leader to save them. Eventually, the leader would die, and Israel would eventually turn away from God. This pattern repeated over and over for generations. But, long before the Israelites ever entered into the promised land, Moses explained God's heart for the Israelites. In verse 12 of Deuteronomy 28, Moses explained their reward for following God: "The Lord will open the heavens, the storehouse of his bounty, to send rain on your land in season and to bless all the work of your hands. You will lend to many nations but will borrow from none." Then, in verse 27, Moses uses sobering words to explain the consequence for *not* following God: "The Lord will cause you to be defeated before your enemies. You will come at them from one direction but flee from them in seven, and you will become a thing of horror to all the kingdoms on earth."

By the time I got to the major prophets, I was deeply aware of the Israelites' struggle to be faithful to God. From Isaiah to Jeremiah to Ezekiel, over hundreds of years, the prophets challenged Israel to repent. I saw a God who cared deeply for His people—and yet the Israelites rebelled. I saw a God who went to great lengths to warn His people about the consequences of rejecting His protection. But the Israelites kept wanting to live life on their terms, not God's. Joel 2:12–13 captures God's heart for his people so clearly and concisely:

> "Even now," declares the Lord, "Return to me with all your heart with fasting and weeping and mourning. Rend your heart and not your garments. Return to the

Lord your God for he is gracious and compassionate, slow to anger and abounding in love, and he relents from sending calamity."

It was during the silence of those late nights reading the Bible that my heart finally began to soften. God was faithful to Israel, and even in my mess, God was being faithful to me, too. I leaned back in my chair and thought, *For hundreds of years, God sent prophet after prophet to warn His people and give them a chance to trust Him. But they wanted life on their terms.* As this revelation washed over me, I

> **It is only when we believe God is good and faithful that we can trust Him to be King of our Life.**

was finally able to answer my burning question: *Can I trust God? Yes. Can I trust Him with everything? Absolutely.*

As I began to walk with a new level of trust in God's love for me and His faithfulness, a new battlefield began to emerge almost immediately in my mind. I went from putting God on trial to putting myself on trial. With each step of faith that I took, I began to unravel all the excuses and rationalizations that I made for my past behavior. I knew intellectually that God forgave me, but I couldn't seem to forgive myself. I found myself trapped in a cycle of shame that felt inescapable. It was like I had gone from the frying pan into the fryer. No matter how much I prayed or journaled, I just couldn't shake the overwhelming sense of guilt about how recklessly I had lived my life in my twenties. Being a good husband was becoming increasingly harder as the demands of parenting ramped up. In the weeks that followed, my shame became almost crippling. And yet, in the depth of my despair, I had no idea that Jesus was about to set the record straight.

It was a Sunday morning in March 2016, and Pastor Mark was wrapping up his message from that morning.

"Peter had great courage to step out of the boat and walk toward Jesus," he preached. "But when he took his eyes off Jesus and focused on the waves, he began to sink."

I'd heard this story a hundred times in my life, but that morning it hit differently. *That's me!* I thought. *I look at all the challenges and forget Jesus is with me. I need to focus only on Him.*

"Then Jesus said to Peter, 'You of little faith; why did you doubt?'" Pastor Mark continued. "Most of us, when we read these verses, think Jesus is angry. But as I read these verses, I think Jesus is actually speaking in tenderness, like a good shepherd would speak to his sheep. I can imagine his tone being gentle and uplifting—almost as if he were saying, 'You were doing so well walking on the water! Why did you take your eyes off of me?'"

As the words came out of Pastor Mark's mouth, tears welled up in my eyes. *Could Your heart really be this tender toward me, Jesus?*

"I've asked a few of the elders to come up to the front," Pastor Mark went on. "If you would like to be prayed for, please come forward. All they will do is take the oil and make the symbol of the cross on your forehead and pray for you."

Feeling a stirring in my heart, I walked toward the front along with most of the church. When my turn came, an elderly couple waved me toward them. I'd never met them before. The man was soft-spoken, and it was very hard to hear him. As he made the cross on my forehead and prayed for me, I prayed, too. *Would You help me to remember Your tenderness toward me, Jesus?*

As I turned to walk back to my seat, the man's wife grabbed my arm with such force that it stopped me in my tracks. It felt like I'd walked into a brick wall. *How could such a small woman grab me with such jarring force?* I thought. I turned to face this stranger and noticed her eyes radiating with extreme kindness and fierceness. It felt like I was looking straight into the eyes of Jesus.

Before another thought could cross my mind, this woman who I had never spoken to before and knew nothing of my life, looked into my eyes and with great conviction said: "My beloved, you are a man after my own heart."

Time stood still. Each of these words pointed back to my namesake, King David. I couldn't look away as she continued.

"Don't you know that I have completely forgiven you?"

In an instant I was undone as the words of Jesus washed over me. Amid my battle against shame that I was both fighting and losing, Jesus stepped in to set the record straight. The King of the Universe stepped into the battle and declared me *not guilty*. In an instant, the battle was won. To my amazement, that wasn't the end of what the woman had to say.

Then the woman spoke a final sentence. "I have great plans for you."

I was shocked, given my past behavior, that Jesus would still have a future for me. But in the stillness of the moment, I remembered that these were the same words my mom had heard when I was in the emergency room as an infant fighting for my life. Awe swept over me.

> **The instant we repent, Jesus forgives. There's nothing in our past that is too much for the Love of Jesus.**

As I walked back to my seat, I replayed the words spoken over me and prayed quietly. *Jesus, today You rescued me from my shame. I finally understand what You mean when the Scriptures say there is nothing that can separate us from Your love—no sins, no past failures. Nothing can separate us from Your love.* In that moment, I felt like I had arrived at the summit of my faith. Over the next few months, though, I would learn I had actually only arrived at the trailhead. The foundation of my faith was being repoured, and my God would faithfully complete His work. But the next few months would bring out the worst in me, even as I tried with all I had to be more like Jesus.

Chapter 6

BUCKLING UNDER PRESSURE

Jesus had met me where I was and in an instant, the shame of my youth was wiped away. Even though I had powerfully experienced the healing power of Jesus in my story, my professional life was still a mess. Despite this incredible gift from Jesus, I still equated my value as a man to my success at work. All it took was my second project drifting from "at risk" to "call the fire trucks," and I once again fought for my significance instead of trusting Jesus through the valley. Only this time, I'd catch an unmistakable glimpse of what I was allowing to happen.

We were celebrating my dad's 62nd birthday early in the spring of 2016 on a Saturday morning. After putting in a full week of work at her job, Caitlin was racing around the house, preparing everything for the party while keeping our energetic, eighteen-month-old son Joshua in tow. It was a difficult solo juggling act, given that I was hunkered down in my office working with my team on a software installation that was moving at a glacial pace. We were already weeks behind schedule and the stress was mounting for everyone. I'd been asked to join the Saturday call and get things back on track, which was all I wanted. I was sure we'd be finished before my dad arrived for the celebration, but I was wrong. The meeting was still in full swing when the doorbell rang at noon.

I turned off my computer camera and raced downstairs to greet my mom and dad with quick hello hugs. Caitlin and Joshua were still in full welcome mode when I told my dad, "Happy Birthday. I'm on a call that is running long, but I should be done soon." I took a mental snapshot of him standing there casually in his blue button-down shirt, jeans, and sneakers, nodding with a sad, knowing smile. He'd perfected the early Saturday business call when I was a child, so I understood the message of his nod. He meant: "I'm proud of you, son. I forgive you for missing the start of my party. This is just what successful men do." I nodded back with a half sad smile. Then, undeterred, I bolted back upstairs, confident in my hope that the installation would be done shortly.

After just coming off the high of getting my last project back on track, I wasn't quite panicking yet. But as the meeting droned on and my dad's party moved forward, my stress mounted. I was trying my best to concentrate on the dialogue between our software engineer, data architect, development manager, senior manager, and project director.

"Did we restart the documentation service before moving on to this next step?" said our data architect.

"Yes," my engineer replied, flipping through his notebook of the installation procedures that he'd followed meticulously.

"I stopped the service, ran the installation step, and restarted the service."

With those steps, the installation should have been complete—but it wasn't. My office was on the second floor and overlooked our open concept dining room and living room. I could hear Joshua delighting everyone with his toddler antics. He'd say something adorable and laughter would erupt. I tried to ignore the joyful banter and focus on the challenge in front of me, but no one on my team seemed to be able to figure out the problem. I rubbed my forehead as anxiety and fear started to creep in. I was letting my dad down while failing to advance my career.

"How can you let this happen?" the senior manager snapped, furious at what he saw as our collective incompetence. He didn't wait for an answer. "We're weeks behind schedule. These development servers must be fully installed today. No excuses. We're not making the client wait any longer. No one is moving until we get this right."

No one dared to groan. Satisfied that his senior manager was adequately whipping us all into shape, the director abruptly dropped off the call to enjoy the rest of his weekend. My mind was racing as I looked at my clock. We'd been on the call for hours and hadn't made any progress. I was about to completely miss my dad's birthday. *Am I really that guy who misses major family celebrations?* I thought. But I knew the answer. I felt suffocated. Everyone on the call was silent, heads down, reviewing their notes. The only sound was the clicking of keyboard keys. My head began to pound as my family's laughter and chatter continued downstairs.

"That's weird," my engineer shot up, clearly on to something. "It's not behaving like it does in our staging server. The two environments are different."

Almost at the exact same time, my wife popped her head in the door. "David, we're going to sing "Happy Birthday" to your dad now and open presents. *Please* come down." I could hear the ache in her voice but only shrugged and waved her off without even taking my eyes off my computer screen. The environments behaving differently signified that our problem was much bigger than we'd originally thought.

About an hour later, Caitlin knocked again. "David," she said quietly, "the party's over now. Your parents have left." She closed the door without waiting for a response this time.

I looked at the clock. It was nearly five in the evening. My heart sank. I was beginning to understand what Jesus meant in Mark 8 when He said: "What good is it for someone to gain the whole world, yet forfeit their soul?"

I'd missed my dad's birthday party, left my wife to do all the work, and failed to acknowledge the longing in her heart for me to be present with our family. Despite spending a tremendous amount of energy rebuilding the foundation of faith, no one from the outside would have thought that I was growing spiritually. I'd raced into chasing after this promotion without a second thought of the price I would have to pay. There was no way to unwind this mistake. The only way was through.

> **We have to believe that our provision comes from Jesus before we can have the courage to set boundaries at work.**

"Let's call it a wrap for the day," our data architect finally said. "I don't know if we're any closer to a solution, but we'll pick back up tomorrow at noon."

In the weeks that followed, weekend calls became the norm as everything we touched broke. We'd fix it, and it would break again. As the project continued to unravel, Caitlin experienced the worst of me. I was unavailable, unhelpful, volatile, and depressed. I didn't even want to be around myself.

And yet I was actually trying really hard to integrate my faith into my work and family. As things deteriorated, I cried out to Jesus in anguish in the same living room where I'd missed my dad's party a few weeks earlier. I prayed: "Love, joy, peace, patience, kindness, goodness . . . all of these fruits of the spirit, and I don't have a single one." My tone darkened from hurt to accusation. "I've been trying to follow You and I'm only getting worse. *Everything* is worse. Where are You?"

It had only been a handful of weeks since that powerful moment in church. I was supposed to be a man after His heart, with great plans for my life. Yet in that moment I believed the exact opposite was true. I thought Jesus was taking me on a journey of success as the world defines it. But He was more concerned with who I was becoming than what I was accomplishing. I did not yet understand that Jesus was teaching me that when we trust Him in the trials, we can have peace even when everything goes wrong. At this time in my life, my faith only worked when everything was going well. And with my life in a tailspin, anger seeped out as I tried to understand where Jesus was in this moment.

I remember one night when Caitlin walked past the kitchen counter after dinner and politely said, "Hey, don't forget to unload the dishwasher." She was just looking for me to meet her halfway and yet with the hurt in my heart overflowing, I struggled to be present for her and Joshua. I nodded absentmindedly and went back to the spinning in my mind as I dwelled on all the problems at work, and just like that, her simple request went to the back of the queue—and it was a very long queue. I walked upstairs to try and make a little more progress on my work. As I came back downstairs, Caitlin saw that I had yet again ignored her request to unload the dishwasher.

"David, this is the *fourth* time I've asked you to unload the dishwasher—the *fourth* time—and it's still full!"

"I know!" I snapped. "Sorry, I'll do it before I go to bed." Except I wasn't really sorry, and I didn't end up following through—on this or *anything* Caitlin needed from me. The toxic garbage in my heart was leaking out on everyone around me. I was poisoning the person I loved most in the world and to whom I was supposed to be giving my best.

As I walked downstairs the next morning, I walked right past the kitchen, not even noticing the dishwasher had been unloaded. I was oblivious and instead slumped down on the couch like a depressed teen. Caitlin tried to engage me in conversation, but as usual I wasn't really there. After multiple failed attempts to awaken me from my stupor, Caitlin hit a boiling point.

"David!" She clapped her hands, as if she were trying to bring me out of a trance. "You need to hear me!" she shouted. "This is not okay. *You* are not okay. You need help." Coming from my typically calm and collected wife, the message was crystal clear.

"Caitlin, I'm trying my best," I snapped back. "I'm trying to provide for our family. If you'd just reduce your hours at work, we'd be okay." Except we weren't okay. I was blaming her for the mess I'd created. I wasn't the man she'd said yes to at the altar. I was coming undone.

As the intensity at home grew, Pastor Mark's men's group became a lifeline. The man I once pitied for being in the trenches was now my companion. My world was unraveling. As I laid my struggles before the men sitting around the table, there was compassion and gentleness.

As each of the guys went around the table offering encouragement, my pastor spoke up: "David, I'm hearing you talk and there's no doubt that these circumstances are hard. I see your hurt and feel your pain. But I just get the sense that this isn't a mistake."

I did a double take. *Did I hear that right?* I thought. *My wise and seasoned pastor just said, 'This isn't a mistake'?* And there it was. Salt in the wound. Week after week, as I gave my ever more depressing updates to the men sitting around the table, Pastor Mark would pipe up and remind me, "David, this isn't a mistake." I felt like a toddler being force-fed boiled broccoli.

Spring turned into summer, and my struggles at work continued to exact a heavy price on every aspect of my life. I had no clue there was another way. I felt trapped, and my prayers were singularly focused on asking God to show up and fix my circumstances. I had no idea that the better prayer was to ask God to help me grow stronger in my faith to meet those challenges. I was trying to apply human logic to the Kingdom of God because I didn't yet understand that His definition of success looks, feels, and tastes very different than ours. I journaled. I prayed. I cried. But I still felt as if failure was all around me. And yet in this pain, I was reminded of the prayer that I prayed in West Virginia for work to be hard so that it would draw me toward Him. I could see Jesus at work protecting me from failure and drawing me toward Him, but what I really wanted was mountaintop success with the blessing of Jesus at my back, propelling me forward. My honest prayer was being answered, just not on my terms. Anger mixed with confusion as I poured out the pain before Jesus. I cried for help from the depth of my heart:

Jesus,

You say You won't give us more than we can handle, but I can't remember a time so terrible as this. I feel like I am falling flat on my face. Every front is a battleground, and I am losing. I feel like You're nowhere to be found. I can't even find the desire in my heart to come to You. I'm overwhelmed and it feels like the darkness is closing in. It feels like my body is failing me. From my eyes to my head to my chest. I know You've spoken great plans to me, but this feels more like death than life. There is nothing left. I don't see You, I don't feel You. I'm just so weary.

I longed for the pain to go away and to feel the healing effect of Jesus's presence like I had experienced at church on that Sunday. But all I felt was frustration and pain. I didn't yet understand that Jesus was calling me deeper. He was calling me to become stronger and more resilient so that I could handle bigger challenges. Ever so slowly, the anger and sorrow began to give way as hope finally began to emerge. I journaled:

Jesus,

I feel like the pressure is slowly starting to come off. This season has taken me to the limit, but I know that You were faithful and that You are faithful. I clung on to the words You gave me and trusted You. Today I saw You move and save us yet again. I get the sense that this hardship and heartache have been preparing me for something that You are stirring in my heart for a reason. My heart is open, my hands are open; I want to be the man that You have called me to be.

Amid these challenges, Jesus was present, even in what I thought was silence. Like a physical therapist, He was working on my range of motion, trying to help my faith grow. Slowly, I started to see small moments of the day differently—and started to invite Jesus into those moments. I was learning to trust Him and let Him lead me. Without really noticing it, even my insignificant habits started to change. Each time fear took hold of me and the urgency of the moment gripped my chest, I mustered up all my courage and did what was counter to every ounce of my professional training. I stopped and went outside.

In the intensity of the moment, I walked outside to see the sky and inhale the fresh air all around me. It was a small act of defiance. As if by going outside, I was leaving behind culture's definition of success and embracing the Kingdom of God. In the office everything was falling apart but out in the open air, the trees, animals, and sky remained perfectly serene. *Everything is just fine out here*, I'd remind myself. *The sun still rises, the rain still falls, and the earth is still spinning.*

I began to recognize that even though my world felt out of control, Jesus was still fully in control. My trust in Him was growing deeper.

> **There are only two ways to respond to deep pain: numb out until we stop hurting or trust Jesus to use the pain for our good.**

There was one saving grace. In those days, Joshua was happy as could be tucked into a stroller for long walks. Our neighborhood was built on a series of canals and lined with trees. Each weekend, I would load Joshua into the stroller and get out in the fresh air. I would lay down my anxiety at the foot of Jesus and ask Him to step into these broken places and give me strength. There was something about moving my feet, being in nature, and praying that seemed to all work in unison. My problems didn't miraculously go away, but I became a little bit stronger each day as I began to trade my anxiety for Jesus's peace.

Little by little, my team at work went from completely doomed to struggling. Eventually, the perception across the firm shifted as our partners realized that this wasn't a mismanaged project but an exceptionally hard one. After many months of work, we finally made it to our go live date and the system worked. The days after we went live were still harrowing, but we made it work. In that valley, I could have interpreted everything that I saw, felt, and experienced as factual evidence that Jesus wasn't with me. And I would have believed the lie of the enemy. Instead, I leaned solely on Jesus in the valley. There were many long and challenging days ahead, but for the first time in my professional life, I began to see a new way to live. A way that was anchored in trusting Jesus with each of life's moments. Just like Pastor Mark had taught me.

A few weeks later, in May 2016, my promotion finally came through, and I became one of the youngest senior managers at the firm. The praise and admiration instantly came pouring in from my colleagues. But no one saw the cost I had paid for this promotion. Yes, I was happy about my new job. But as I looked around the office, I felt hollow. Was this really what I wanted for my life? I was beginning to rethink my definition of success.

Chapter 7

GOD LOVES ME, EVEN AT MY WORST!

In the days that followed my promotion, I was exhausted. I had never expended so much effort in my entire life simply to avoid failure. While I wasn't working around the clock anymore, I had far from recovered from these trying months. It was now August 2016, and Caitlin and I were in high spirits as we geared up to celebrate my brother's wedding. We were both hoping the event would provide a welcome getaway from all the stress. It would be a chance for us to rejuvenate and reconnect after months of strain.

My brother Leo was in his early twenties and already the CEO of an e-commerce platform. He'd just sold off one of the company's divisions to a large multinational in Chicago and didn't show any signs of slowing down. He was charismatic, energetic, and loved by all. His soon-to-be wife, Samantha, matched him bit for bit with her charisma, energy, and passion. The hotel estate they chose for the wedding was as expansive as it was expensive. The grounds of the hotel covered three thousand acres and sat at the foothills of the Blue Ridge Mountains. The property was home to a ten-acre lake and historic ruins. It was a resort that had it all and the rooms at the venue were about $400 per night—outside what Caitlin and I wanted to spend at the time. We also had Joshua in tow, so we opted to stay at a Hampton Inn about twenty minutes away. I was the best man but desperately needed to put some points on the board with Caitlin. Yet almost from the start, it became clear that my duty to my brother would make this difficult. After the rehearsal dinner, my brother asked me to spend time with him. I mentioned this to Caitlin, and her eyes shot me a you're-still-not-okay message. Like me, she was exhausted. She desperately needed a break.

"David, I've been all alone taking care of Joshua night after night for months! I'm exhausted and need your help."

When I let my brother know that I was going home after the rehearsal dinner, his expression made it clear how much I'd disappointed him. I felt terribly conflicted. The next morning, my father pulled me aside. "I heard from your brother that you went home early last night."

"Yes, I went home *early*," I said sarcastically, making air quotes with my fingers around the word *early*. "I needed to support my wife and son, who is still not sleeping through the night. We're exhausted."

With the tension rising, my father doubled down. "You know this week is very important for your brother. You're his best man, David. You let him down. You have to do better." The rebuke was harsh, and I was depleted. I felt like I'd just been sucker punched.

As I walked back over to Caitlin, she asked, "What was that all about?"

"Oh, you know," I replied, pretending to be lighthearted. "I'm not doing enough as the best man. I'm a bad son. I'm letting everyone down."

"You gotta be kidding me," Caitlin said as she rolled her eyes.

From the outside, it looked like I'd handled the exchange well. On the inside, however, I was in a wreck. *The blows at work are one thing. I know I've missed the mark with Caitlin—now, my family, too?* I felt like failure was washing over my identity again. Even when I was trying to walk in my faith, I wasn't getting it right. My despair was giving way to bitterness and a toxic anger was churning in my heart, ready to explode like a grenade.

The wedding was beautiful, and thankfully I was able to keep it together. The reception was held deep in the estate, inside the historic ruins, which were surrounded by perfectly manicured gardens and elegant fountains reminiscent of the Victorian age. It was enchanting. As we walked through this idyllic setting to the reception area, the excitement was palpable. Everything was going according to plan. Dinner was delicious. The speeches and toasts were iconic. After dinner, everyone raced to the dance floor, enjoying the music, mixed drinks, and a cool autumn evening under the stars. But thirty minutes in, the music abruptly stopped. I swung around in my chair to see what had happened and grabbed Caitlin's arm. "Oh no! It looks like Samantha fell."

As a physician's assistant, Caitlin sprang into action, assessing the injured bride like a pro. "Samantha, what happened?"

"I don't know," the bride replied, writhing in agony. "I was dancing with my brother and then I heard something pop."

With a concerned look, Caitlin tried to get Samantha to her feet, but it was clear she couldn't put any weight on her ankle, which had ballooned to a size beyond what seemed humanly possible.

Caitlin came back to our table deeply concerned. "David, Samantha's ankle is injured. It's swelling up like a balloon and she can't put any pressure on it."

As I looked around, I began to realize just how serious her injury was. *Could an ambulance even make it this far into the estate? Even the parking lot isn't close by,* I thought.

My questions was soon answered when somehow, about twenty minutes later, an ambulance arrived and backed up to the dance floor; the bride was loaded on to the stretcher in her wedding gown and taken to the hospital.

The guests looked at each other, confused. The music started back up at half volume, but the dance floor remained empty. Slowly and unnaturally, the party came to an end. My brother and now sister-in-law were despondent. Their beautiful celebration had turned into a medical emergency. In an alternate universe, I would have had the energy to rise to the occasion and comfort them when they needed me most. But I'd spent all my energy at work, and my heart was set on repairing the damage between me and Caitlin. As the dance floor emptied out, Caitlin whispered to me, "David, I think it's time to get Joshua home for bed." She paused before she continued. "I think the night is over and I can barely keep my eyes open."

Looking out at the emptying reception area, I nodded in agreement. "Why don't you start loading Joshua into the car," I said in a melancholy tone, "and I'll start saying goodbyes to everyone."

The weight of everything was hitting me like a brick. A weekend away had turned into a stressful event. After saying my final goodbyes, I started walking toward the parking lot.

"Where are you going?" my dad called out, his tone both perplexed and frustrated.

With exhaustion now taking its full effect, I thought, *How in the world does he not know that I'm heading to the parking lot?*

"Back to the hotel with Caitlin and Joshua," I replied bluntly.

"Oh, I don't think so, David," my dad shot back. "Your brother needs you even more right now."

Just like that, the hurt and rejection from the last few months overwhelmed my coping mechanisms. "Samantha is hurt, dad. The wedding is *over*," I blurted out in a tone of utter disrespect. "I'm going back to the hotel. I have a baby and a wife I need to take care of."

"You are *not* going to abandon your brother in his time of need, David!"

I was trying to hold it all together but snapped and started shouting a slew of profanities as I continued to head for the parking lot. "Take one last good look at me, dad. I'm done. You will never see my face again. I'm done with you. I'm done with this family. I'm done forever."

Like a running back scrambling to get a fumbled football, I could sense my body almost immediately trying to grab back each word. In hindsight, my volcanic explosion was inevitable. I'd been trying to process my pain and sadness for months in my journal, but it kept bubbling back up. I could not seem to release it. And as the pressure built, my hurt poured out on the people who I loved most in the world. That night, my dad got a look at the absolute worst in me. It was one of the lowest points in my life and when I think about it now, it still brings me to tears. But today, when I reflect on this devastating moment of failure in my past, I am reminded of how little I still understood God's love back then. In modern cancel culture, it's easy to mistakenly think that Jesus shuns us when we make mistakes. But Paul, who once violently persecuted the followers of Jesus with the utmost zeal, would experience this love and forgiveness from Jesus and years later would write in Romans 8:38–39: "For I am convinced that neither death nor life, neither angels nor demons neither the present nor the future, nor any powers, neither height nor depth, nor anything else in all creation, will be able to separate us from the love of God that is in Christ Jesus our Lord."

Jesus had never abandoned me, even at my worst. He was not looking for a big moment of failure to write me off. Instead, He was whispering, "Get up. This isn't the end; we have further to go."

By the time I arrived at the car, I felt defeated. I had allowed the absolute worst of me and my words to be spoken to my father, a person I was supposed to show the utmost honor toward. As I neared Caitlin, I told her what happened.

Stunned, she replied, "Are you okay?"

> **Jesus is more concerned with who we are becoming than what we've done.**

She knew I wasn't. But I mustered all the strength I had left to say, "I think so, but I know that I have to help my brother."

My faith had finally broken through my rage and anger. Despite my brokenness, I got back up to put the pieces back together. In a generous act of compassion, Caitlin quietly nodded and said, "I understand."

Our drive back to the hotel was quiet. I said goodnight and headed back to the wedding venue. In the hours that followed,

I had the chance to care for my brother and sister-in-law as they emerged from the hospital. I was surprised with how many little things they needed help with that night to get settled.

The next morning, I found my dad at the breakfast table and pulled him aside. I took a deep breath. "I'm really sorry about what I said to you last night. You're my father and talking to you with such disrespect was completely out of line." I paused as I tried to gain my composure. "You were right. Leo and Samantha needed my help."

Without missing a beat, my dad replied, "I know you're under a lot of stress. I forgive you. I'm really glad you were able to help them."

It had been more than eight months since I'd written my first journal entry, but after this life-altering event, journal writing became a primary tool for working through my heartache.

> Jesus,
>
> What am I supposed to see in this season? I can feel bitterness creeping in. You speak of great things, yet it seems like I'm always in this uphill battle. There's no greatness in these moments. I know that only a few days have passed, but You feel so far away. Would You help me to trust You? Would You bring joy and gratefulness back into my heart and show me how blessed I am?

Over the next few months, I continued to process my oversize emotions and confusion in the pages of my journal: "I feel like I'm pouring clean and good water into my heart, but only junk is coming out. What is going on with me?" It felt like I was losing ground, but in truth, Jesus was just sweeping out all the garbage that had accumulated in my heart. After months of journaling, praying, and working through everything, I came to the realization that the cost of being a senior manager at the firm was not worth more than my spiritual health and my family. I knew my time at the firm was over.

Chapter 8

TWO COMPETING TRUTHS

In November 2016, I quit the firm without anything else lined up. Unfortunately, the job market for my consulting and project management skill set was nearly nonexistent. My dad, who had received the brunt of my anger and frustration only a few months earlier, stepped in and offered me a job at his consulting firm. I had dishonored and wronged him, yet he was full of compassion and mercy. On a cool Saturday morning, he came over and I saw the heart of Jesus modeled by my dad.

"David, I've been thinking. My consulting practice is growing, and I think it might really benefit from your expertise. I think you'd make a great partner." He took a slight pause and looked me straight in the eyes before delivering the question. "Would you consider joining me?"

My response was enthusiastic and instantaneous. "Dad, that's a dream come true. I'd love to work with you."

Before starting with my dad, both Caitlin and I agreed that it would be good for me to take a few days to get away, decompress, and regroup after all the stress from working at the firm. As I looked at all the different ways I could blow off some steam, hiking seemed like the only healthy option. I had done a handful of shorter hikes prior to meeting Caitlin and loved the feeling of accomplishment when I finished a hike. Caitlin's love of hiking had furthered my experience and enjoyment on the trails. So I booked a cabin at the quiet trailhead of Grandfather Mountain in North Carolina for mid-November.

At best I was a novice hiker, so I knew the 1,700 feet of elevation gain would definitely wear me out. By the time that I had arrived at the trailhead, a soft, gentle rain was falling, which had apparently deterred all other hikers. On a cool fall day with the rain slowly falling, I found myself completely alone on the trail. But, in that moment, it felt like the rainfall somehow matched the somber, weary state of my heart. The rain made the climb more challenging and slower as I took extra care not to slip on the steep ascent of Grandfather Mountain.

> **We all have sacred places that help us strip away the cares of the world. Make space to find yours.**

As I finally reached the summit after about a two-and-a-half-hours-long climb, the relentless, bone-chilling November rain became magnified by gusty winds. I was so wet and cold, I started shaking. Quickly swapping out my wet shirt for a heavier jacket I'd brought in my backpack, I decided not to linger. My descent back down the mountain was as grueling as my ascent, and when I walked back to my cabin after an early dinner, I collapsed in bed. It felt like I'd left everything on the mountain, emptying my spirit and body on this unrelenting hike. Lying in bed, I could feel blood rushing through my veins, almost as if a new supply of fresh blood was filling my body back up. I was completely exhausted but totally exhilarated.

The next day, I mustered up my remaining strength and hiked Mount Mitchell, an eleven-mile trail with a four-thousand-foot elevation gain. As I walked up this second mountain, my feet moved slowly and my heart raced, but my mind was quiet. All my fears and anxieties fell away as I made my way up the mountain. I was fully present in the moment and felt at peace. And while it probably wasn't what Luke meant when he said, "Jesus often slipped away to be alone so he could pray," hiking was proving to be a powerful way for me to slip away and pray.

As I got back on the plane to go home that evening, I realized that hiking had been the perfect way to end this season of my life. And despite heading back home physically tired, I felt a little bit more whole. I'd headed to the mountains in a state of spiritual depletion and had come back rejuvenated.

I started work with my dad the following week. Despite arriving fresh and ready for this new chapter of my life, I was not prepared for the professional pivot my dad had to make shortly after I joined his consulting firm. His firm's pipeline of new clients was slowing down. There weren't any outside factors or reasons to explain the slowdown. In hindsight, I can now see that Jesus was leading us down a different path. My hope of working alongside my dad as a partner was about to give way to an adventure of a lifetime. Just six weeks into my new role, my dad pulled me aside at the office to talk about the progress of a company that he'd co-founded a year earlier with two of his longtime colleagues, Ben and Phil. It was called Adaptive Technologies, and the business model was built around licensing and commercializing disruptive technologies from global companies. The company's thesis was that start-ups are better suited for the commercialization of new ideas than big companies because there is less red tape.

"David, I know things are tough right now in the consultancy practice. But Adaptive Technologies is nearing an inflection point. There are some critical meetings coming up next week and I'd like you to attend."

The following week, I hopped in the car with my dad for the three-hour drive to the west coast of Florida. Always focused on optimal productivity, my dad asked me to drive so he could work. As we neared Fort Myers, he told me, "Today's meeting is with Tim and his family office. Tim has recently retired as CEO of a major Fortune 50 company. He is thinking about creating a partnership with Adaptive Technologies."

Impressed, I asked, "How big is their family office?"

"Right now, there about nine people, but their marketing and operational strength really is a perfect complement to our capabilities."

My dad explained that Ben and Phil, his cofounders, would be part of the leadership team. Ben, a charismatic strategist, had developed a very strong relationship with a major Fortune 50 company and secured a global license to one of their most disruptive innovations. Ben would lead the major commercial efforts, and Phil would lead the financing and scientific efforts. My dad would be the chief operating officer. Each partner brought years of unique expertise to the table. They offered a perfect blend of strategic thinking, strong people skills, stellar execution, and scientific expertise. Together, they were a force to be reckoned with.

As we pulled into the condo, I realized this would be a less formal environment than I was used to. We were actually meeting in the condo community's clubhouse, lushly decorated with a

Tommy Bahama–Caribbean vibe. Instead of the sterile conference rooms that I had become accustomed to, plush couches invited everyone to relax. It felt like an odd place to explore such an important strategic partnership. Despite the casual setting, though, I was keenly aware that the caliber of people in the room was off the charts.

Ben started the meeting and spoke for about forty-five minutes explaining to the group of fifteen people all the innovations that Adaptive Technologies had analyzed. After explaining their evaluation methodology and rationale for rejecting the other technologies, Ben pivoted as he explained, "It is clear that GreenWave is head and shoulders above the rest. Its groundbreaking technology can deliver unprecedented value across a range of industries, from consumer products to automotive to just about any fiber-based material."

As Ben's words sunk in, I could see the excitement building in the room. This was a chance to do good and build a successful business. Ben continued. "We now have a global license to progress the technology. Our initial modeling indicates that GreenWave could be a one-billion-dollar company over the next five to seven years."

Seamlessly, my dad picked up where Ben left off. "Over the last year, we've been progressing the tests in the lab and believe that the technology is now in a place where we are ready to scale."

"We're just now exiting the in-depth R&D phase," Ben weighed in. "Going forward, GreenWave is going to need a lot more care and feeding."

As the morning updates came to a close, lunch was brought in, and I saw Tim and his brother Wes, also a retired executive, sitting by themselves by the pool. *This is a once-in-a-lifetime opportunity,* I thought. *These men are so successful. I could learn so much from them*. I mustered up all my courage, approached them, and asked if I could join them for lunch. Without missing a beat, they welcomed me to their table. Lunch was everything I'd hoped—informational and inspiring. As we wrapped up, I thanked them for allowing me to sit with them and took my seat at the back of the room.

After lunch, the conversation moved to the big questions: What would the partnership look like? How much additional fundraising would be needed? Who would take on the main roles in the company?

Eventually, Tim abruptly stopped the conversation. "So who is really working full-time on all this?"

He was keying into the fundamental challenge of the business. Everyone was working on Adaptive Technologies part-time, except for Ben. Tim looked at my dad and said, "You have a consulting practice and you're supporting Ben. What's your priority?"

Without missing a beat, my dad looked Tim in the eyes. "If you guys came on board, I'd move to full-time and close down my consulting firm."

I felt like I had just been sucker punched. I could feel adrenaline surging through my body as my heart rate began to climb. *How could he do this to me? We're supposed to be partners.* Just like my brother's wedding, I could feel the rage and darkness rising up inside of me. I'd done a lot of spiritual work since then and had more control over my emotions. My desire to honor Jesus was now greater than my desire to say what I felt. A few minutes later, the team took a fifteen-minute break and I made a beeline for my dad. I could tell that I'd calmed my body down enough to speak to him in a civil tone. We found a quiet spot outside of the meeting room and I said, "I can't believe you said you were going to shut down the consulting practice without even talking to me."

"I need to do what I think is best for us, and this is where we need to be," my dad replied calmly.

"This isn't what I agreed to, dad."

"You're just going to have to trust me, David." And with that he calmly walked away.

In the weeks that followed, my dad carved out a role for me at Adaptive Technologies. It would involve the impressive title of vice president—and a pay cut. I would also go from being number two at my dad's consulting firm to bottom of the rung at Adaptive Technologies. Though the opportunity seemed huge, it felt like a step backward for me professionally.

It had been less than a year since Jesus had led me through a series of challenges to learn how to trust Him. I still struggled, but I was slowly opening my heart and letting Him steer my life. While I was still a ways off from complete surrender, I was beginning to learn how to walk by faith. Though the circumstances of life still led me to feel unloved and undervalued, Jesus had begun a deep work in my heart and I was beginning to walk differently.

Chapter 9

GIVING AND GROWING IN FAITH

It was the first quarter of 2017, and I was the vice president of operations at Adaptive Technologies. While my title sounded impressive, my workload was light—nothing close to my responsibilities at the firm. I took meeting notes, tracked action items, and created project schedules—all entry-level tasks. I wondered how my talents and experience could be so overlooked and underutilized. I had now been journaling for more than a year and as my self-doubts and sadness mounted, I opened my journal and poured out my hurt and confusion onto the page, trying to be grateful for my new position:

Jesus,

I am so grateful that You brought me to Adaptive Technologies, a place where I can recover. I can see how the last year of work has prepared me for the challenges and uncertainty here. I feel like I've grown from these trials and my hope for the future is not in my ability, but in You.

My heart was starting to align with the standards of Scripture instead of the world's definition of success. While I had spent a lot of time focusing on improving my emotions and behavior, there was one area that I hadn't yet trusted Jesus with: my finances. As I read through the Holy Scriptures, I began to realize that I thought about *my* money with a scarcity mindset. I felt like I never had enough money to live the type of lifestyle I wanted. Somehow my scarcity mindset had subtly turned into a type of hidden greed. Eventually, my heart began to cry out to be faithful to Jesus with our finances. I began praying that we'd be able to tithe, which traditionally is referred to as giving 10 percent of your income back to God. At the time, I had no idea that tithing would actually help reorient my heart and remind me that my provision comes from Jesus. As was my practice, I wrote in my journal:

Jesus,

My heart is open. My hands are open. I want to be the man that You called me to be. I guess it's what's next that scares me. So I ask that You'll create a moment where Caitlin and I can talk about finances so we can be deliberate about tithing and be faithful to You financially. I want to trust in You for our provision. I want to follow You, but I am still scared that it means You'll ask more of me than I can give. Help me to remember that You are good and that You love me.

It took eight months before I finally built up enough courage to talk with Caitlin about it. As Caitlin sat down on the couch in our living room one Saturday afternoon, I approached the topic with her. I started awkwardly. "Caitlin, I've been thinking. My new job at Adaptive Technologies marks a new season in our lives. I know we're not where we want to be financially, but I was thinking that we should start giving more to the church." I paused to read Caitlin's body language. We both brought in around the same amount of money, so this really was a joint decision.

Caitlin hesitated. "We're already giving a small car payment to the church," she said. "How much more did you want to give?"

I took a deep breath and mustered all the courage I had as I said, "I want to take a step toward giving ten percent."

Caitlin sighed and said, "That's a lot of money."

"I know, but we have a little extra right now and I really think we should honor God with it."

"I'm not excited about this," Caitlin said, "but I'll sleep on it and let you know in the morning."

"I really appreciate your willingness to sit in this moment with me. Thank you, Caitlin."

The next day, she agreed, and we took a major step forward in getting closer to a full tithe. We had come a long way from our early awkward days of attending church. We had finally created a beachhead in our finances through which we could begin to trust Jesus. In the years to come, this beachhead would grow into something much bigger. This is the momentum that exists with faith. We start small and keep challenging ourselves to take the next step. All throughout the Scriptures, we see that our God is a God who sees the heart.

Despite my spiritual progress, I still found myself struggling as I continued to be overlooked at work. At Adaptive Technologies, everyone worked from home long before the COVID pandemic. We came together monthly in Fort Myers to discuss our progress and outline priorities of the month. As the founders sat around the cozy living room, Ben asked for the team's support. "These next few months are going to be critical for GreenWave," he explained. "We really need *everyone's* help."

In the breaks throughout the day, I watched Ben ask team member after team member to lean in and support the work that lay ahead. But he never approached me. *What about me?* I wondered, feeling overlooked and underappreciated. Just as I was about to let myself spiral into an endless cycle of negativity, a thought whispered in my mind: *Don't you remember I have great plans for you?*

In that moment, I had a chance to choose which reality I would believe. I could either let the facts on the ground make me feel unwanted or believe that Jesus had a plan for me. I chose the latter and fought against my feelings of hurt. That night, I would journal:

Jesus,

Thank You for speaking to my heart today. In the meeting as they were talking about the plans for the people, I was so hurt. It was like I didn't even exist. And I just felt like You softly whispered: *Don't you remember that I have plans for you?* And You reminded me of your promise. I could even see how the words I spoke later in the meeting were from You and not out of my brokenness. So I thank You that I am growing. Even just last month, this would have broken me. Thank You for what You're doing in my heart.

It was in these moments of both quiet and challenge that I was able to be more present and attune myself to Caitlin's heart. With work at a manageable pace, I was able to fully enjoy my family more. So when Caitlin's parents, who were now visiting during the winter months, invited us to the beach, we were thrilled. It was a delight to watch our boy experience sand for the first time. He flung it everywhere in pure joy. It was another one of those memorable parenting moments infused with our child's zest for life. It was during these days that Caitlin and I began talking about growing our family. I had always wanted two kids and thought the closer we could keep the age gap, the better friends they would become. In the months that would follow, we conceived our second son, Ezra.

> **Pain alerts us to the places that haven't yet been healed by Jesus.**

Back at work, the perpetual meeting cadence had us either preparing for a monthly meeting or following up on one. With millions of dollars now invested into this dream, the stakes were high. Our meetings moved from Florida to our new Chicago headquarters, which Tim's team graciously allowed us to use. Updates were replaced with managing pivotal inflection points to make sure we were hyperfocused on the activities that would drive the business forward. There was one office at the corner of the building, one conference room, and an open space with two couches and an eighty-five-inch TV on one side and a group of desks filling up the other side.

The meeting was packed with fifteen people, and the space was littered with office chairs for those who weren't fortunate enough to grab a seat on the couch. I was in a chair toward the back of the room. The meeting moved seamlessly through agenda topics, until it was my dad's turn. Ever focused, he covered his assigned points meticulously with the executive swagger he'd perfected over the years. Finally, it was my turn. I methodically walked the team through the critical path of the schedule I'd been working on, relentlessly flagging all the things that could slow us down. As I finished my update, Tim, ever observant, asked a singular question.

"If building the pilot plant is going to take eighteen months, what do we need to see from the lab to have enough confidence to start construction?"

Slightly caught off guard because my answer had far-reaching implications, I struggled to quickly map out everything in my head. The racing of my heart made it harder to focus and get the right words out, but I managed to keep my composure. "Thanks for the question, Tim. We're seeing great results in the lab to date. Ideally, we would want to test a broader range of raw materials before we finalize the key equipment." Tim, seemingly satisfied by my answer, nodded, and the conversation moved on from my slides. My heart rate began to slow, and a smile crept across my face.

Almost in the same breath, Ben, one of the founding partners, began to yet again explain the need for more help on GreenWave. "From logistics to fundraising to strategic planning, we could really use more help. If anyone has any extra bandwidth, it would be great to get your help." At the break, Ben made the rounds and asked others in the room for help. His eyes didn't even glance in my direction. Inside, I was crushed and asked myself, *When will I ever be enough?*

Despite wanting to protect time with my family—and not wanting work to become an idol in my life again—I still looked to those around me to answer the questions burning in my mind: *Am I enough? Do I count? Am I respected?* Each time I was overlooked, the answer felt like no, and I was deeply wounded. Fortunately, I had grown enough spiritually to recognize these wounds in real time. That afternoon, I again worked through the pain in my journal.

> Jesus,
>
> My heart is so angry. I almost always get upset after these meetings because it's like I don't matter, and I don't have a place. These feelings break my heart and so I lay the hurt before You. There's no doubt that You're in control, but this hurt creates anger that poisons my heart. Help me to focus on what's true and the life that You have breathed into me. I see You moving, but for some reason I can't get the hope into my heart. Please help me and open my eyes to what I'm missing.

As the months progressed and the hurt continued, I laid it all at the feet of Jesus. By writing things out, I hoped to keep the pain from poisoning my heart. Jesus was patient as small events kept triggering feelings of not being enough. I'd make strides spiritually, then fall into old patterns. And often in the stillness of the late evening, I would write about this emotional roller-coaster ride:

Jesus,

I feel the hurt and insignificance coming back again. I feel like I am being treated like a child. I hear the lies that I'll end up as insignificant. Would You help me wrap my heart around Your truth? Would You calm this anxiety in my heart? I am trying to follow You and be the man You called me to be. Please help me to live by faith. I see glimpses of what You're doing, but I am so afraid. Would You remind me that before the foundation of the world, You chose me? Would You remind me that I am loved by You and because You chose me, it doesn't matter who rejects me?

> Our walk with Jesus isn't linear like a high-performing stock; it's slow and circular like a spring under tension.

At a July 2017 meeting in Chicago, Ben again asked the team leaders to step up and overlooked me. I could feel the hurt coming again, but now I had tools to deal with it. Silently, I started to pray in the conference room. *Jesus, I refuse to let hurt sink in. I know that You see me. I know that I am Yours. I refuse to feel unwanted and unseen. Help me orient my heart to Your truth.*

The pain didn't disappear, but I was learning to diffuse it before it erupted in anger. I never wanted to lose control again, as I had at my brother's wedding. My spiritual practices of reading the Scriptures, journaling, praying, and tithing were all coming together to help me recognize the hurt and lay it at the feet of Jesus. My faith was in action, and I was gradually becoming a different version of myself—a whole(er) version. Yet even with these incredible steps forward, I still struggled to separate my identity from the world's definition of success. My longing to feel successful made it hard to see the times when I allowed work to rob me of time with the family. At first, I barely recognized these minor incursions because I rationalized the workload as "not as bad as what I had to work at the firm." Yet with each passing week, I didn't just allow more work onto my plate, I welcomed it with open arms.

By now, Caitlin and I were in a rhythm of working hard during the week and using vacations as a way to repair, reconnect, and recover. Fortunately, our next getaway was planned for New York City for a long weekend. Without even realizing it, these getaways had become a lifeline for our marriage.

Chapter 10

LEARNING TO OPEN MY HANDS

Having meticulously prepared every detail of our much-needed September 2017 weekend getaway, Caitlin and I were getting excited. My parents had agreed to take Joshua for the weekend, and we'd booked a great room at an upscale hotel, the Omni Berkshire Place, near Central Park. We had made dinner reservations at several restaurants. I had even purchased tickets to her favorite musical, *The Phantom of the Opera*. She'd never seen the play live on Broadway before. I'd also pushed hard to get ahead on all of my work so I could disconnect and be fully present for my wife. Everything was primed for us to be able to reconnect and speak into each other's hearts. But three days before our flight, I was packing in our bedroom when I heard Caitlin call me downstairs with a hint of concern in her voice.

"Hey, David, could you take a look at this?"

We both stared quietly at the TV, which showed the track of Hurricane Irma heading right toward where we lived in Florida. The storm's satellite image looked as big as the state of Florida itself. My stomach dropped.

"This is really bad, right, David?"

Caitlin was still new to hurricanes, having spent her entire life living up north.

"Yeah, like cancel our trip bad. Ugh!"

We both sat there quietly watching the weather report with dread.

Caitlin broke the silence. "What if we brought Joshua with us to New York?"

This would be our last major trip before Ezra was born, and we both knew how hard those first few months with a newborn would be. A sad smile crept across my face. This would change everything about our weekend together, but at least we'd get away.

"I think we could make that work. I'll try to find a sitter in New York so we can still go to our show."

As the new reality of our upcoming vacation washed over me, I poured out my heartache in my journal:

Jesus,

This continues to be an uphill battle. I am so tired of being pressed in on every side. I know that You are reshaping me and shifting the way I react to challenging times. Yet this feeling of hurt overwhelms me. I guess it is a step forward that I'm not blaming You for the mess. Would You help me to have faith in this moment that what You create is good because You are good?

I was still learning how to surrender my life to Jesus and hadn't yet learned that meant holding my plans with open hands. Despite all my progress, I was still inflexible when life went a different direction than I thought it should. Reluctantly, with Joshua in tow, we flew to New York on Friday night. The hotel was spectacular, but Joshua refused to sleep in the pack and play. On Saturday morning, we awoke sleep-deprived, sluggish, and on edge. *This is literally the exact opposite of what I had pictured,* I thought. I let out an audible sigh. Instead of delighting in my wife and son that day, I was short and grumpy as I kept longing for what could have been.

> **When we hold our plans loosely, we make room for Jesus to do the unexpected.**

On the last day of our three-day trip, we took Joshua to the Statue of Liberty. I hadn't really thought about it until that day, but I realized that this would not only be our last trip as a couple before adding another child to our family, but it would also be the last getaway with just the three of us.

"David, let's get some pictures with Joshua," Caitlin requested.

I smiled and nodded, not thinking much of it. I took a few pictures of Caitlin with Joshua and then we switched. As Caitlin handed my phone back to me, she said, "You've got to take a look at this picture."

Staring at the phone in my hand, my heart swelled. With Joshua perfectly tucked into my side, there I was with my son in front of the Statue of Liberty. *I'll remember this moment forever,* I thought. Having longed to be alone with my wife on this trip, I realized Jesus was leading me to be present for Joshua and Caitlin in a different way. He was leading us to be present together as a family. My heart finally softened, and I was filled with joy, love, and contentment.

We didn't get back to the city until around eight o'clock that evening and still hadn't eaten dinner. Joshua, who wasn't quite three years old, was getting agitated and desperately needed some food and a break. We finally found an opening at a nice Italian restaurant in Times Square and were seated in a very nice semicircle booth in the back corner. Caitlin ordered an Italian salad, and I ordered a chicken parmesan sandwich. Overtired, Joshua continued to be loud and rambunctious, so we decided to do something completely out of character for us as parents: We ordered our son a gigantic banana split. The moment it arrived at the table, peace swept over our corner of the restaurant. Caitlin and I laughed as we watched Joshua inhale his ice cream without taking a single breath. *This is what life is all about,* I thought.

Nothing about this getaway had gone as I'd imagined. And yet, that was the gift. I just wasn't able to see it that way in the moment. I thought Caitlin and I needed to escape and reconnect as a couple, but Jesus had different plans. In His tenderness, He used our agitation, tiredness, and brokenness to show us the true gift of our son, who just loved being with us. Our entertainment that night was watching our son eat a banana split for dinner. These were precious memories. Jesus was showing me His ways were not my ways. If I could find the courage to trust Him in the moment, I could begin to see that His plans, no matter how disruptive, were for my good. We returned home to an undamaged house, even though millions had faced devastation from Hurricane Irma. We were deeply grateful. I realized that I was grumbling about a hard weekend getaway while so many others in Florida were figuring out how to rebuild their lives from scratch.

Chapter 11

BREAKING IN THE TENSION

A few weeks after our family trip to New York, GreenWave's CFO pulled me aside. "David, I know you're always volunteering to help, and I could use your help vetting out all the assumptions that we're making in the financial model."

"I'd love to; I really appreciate the opportunity." Thrilled to be needed, I didn't even slow down to ask Jesus if this was an area where I should focus. Processing my pain with Jesus had become automatic, but I hadn't yet learned how to process opportunities with Him.

Almost immediately it became clear I'd signed up for a much more complex job than I had thought. The main tab of the Excel document had over fifty rows and ten columns of complex formulas. Each cell had a formula that led to another formula. Each tab of the model was predicated on cells from other tabs. There were more tabs than I could count. I dug in and told myself that failure was not an option. I was living in that Excel spreadsheet. I called vendors and asked for quotes to validate our assumptions. I spoke to the engineers to make sure that our design basis had changed. I documented everything so our investors could see the supporting details of our assumptions. It was tedious and menial, but I was resolved to do this work to the best of my growing capability. Over the next few months, I emerged as the owner of the financial model, a task my CFO was glad to hand off to me. I poured over every assumption, quote, and estimate. It was in these moments where work slowly began to creep past the healthy balance line. It was a subtle shift that I failed to notice.

I was finally a key part of the team and more work was added to my plate with each new assignment. It was late 2017, and Caitlin was in her final trimester. Ezra would be arriving just before the new year. Caitlin and I had started to drift apart again as she focused on preparing to welcome our second son and I focused on what I thought was providing for our family. We were dividing and conquering life's daily responsibilities, which felt normal, especially for couples in our modern era. Unknowingly, though, I had used our culture's standard for success and had mistakenly thought we were crushing it. Neither Caitlin nor I had any idea how much we were missing the mark spiritually as a couple. While we thought we were thriving, the Holy Scriptures whispered a different standard. The Scriptures spoke of a standard of us becoming one, and we were more like two people living different lives in the same house. It would take years for us to realize that this wisdom from God's Word was for our protection and for our good.

As I dove deeper into GreenWave's financial model, it quickly became clear that the company would need more money. A lot more than we'd originally thought. As the stress and work kept piling up, I turned to my journal:

> Jesus,
>
> I don't know why this is still a hard season. I feel like I have to work all the time to just keep my head above water. I lack hope and see everything through a glass-half-empty lens. I feel like I continue to take on too much and I am at a loss for words. My heart has been a mess lately. It feels like if I could just make a little more money, Caitlin could work less. I feel like I need Your presence. Would You help me understand why I struggle so much to ask for help?

As Ezra's arrival got closer, the doctors saw that he wasn't growing and began to measure his progress much more closely. After a couple more visits, our doctor decided that it would be best to deliver him three weeks early. It was amid this nervous tension at home and at work that we welcomed Ezra into the world, just days before the new year.

Unlike Joshua's terrifying labor, Ezra's birth went smoothly. But the moment our five-pound-fifteen-ounce son arrived, the mood in the delivery room shifted. As the nurses cleaned him up, I could sense concern as they spoke quietly to each other. They kept retaking our son's vitals and listening to his breathing.

"I'm noticing that your son's respirations are low," the head nurse said to us. "We're going to give him some extra oxygen, just as a precaution." With those simple words, the nurses moved swiftly and efficiently as they prepared Ezra to be taken to the Neonatal Intensive Care Unit (NICU). Our hearts sank as the medical team administered dozens of tests to try to determine what was wrong. We watched as our helpless boy was connected to machines, and tubes were stuck in his nose and throat and an IV in his hand. We were told Ezra's lungs were not fully developed and his heart wall was not closing properly. Our son would be in the NICU for several days, the doctors told us. After Caitlin drifted off to sleep, I curled up in a hospital recliner next to Ezra and began to journal, trusting Jesus with my fears and sorrow.

> Jesus,
>
> I know You are good, and I know that You love me. I know that You have called me to sit in this moment, and I am only able to sit in this moment because I've seen You in move in my life and I know how amazing You are. I'm still scared but I trust You. Would You help see our family through this moment?

After seven days in the NICU, we were finally able to take Ezra home. It took a few weeks but by February, Ezra, who was now two months old, was thriving. By looking at him, you'd never have known that he had spent an entire week in the NICU. We had just gotten the all clear from the last doctor and miraculously Ezra appeared to not have a single lingering side effect. We were amazed and grateful.

On a Saturday afternoon shortly after we got the all clear, I remember Joshua playing quietly as Ezra was napping. Caitlin walked into the living room and sat next to me on the couch. "Joshua has been such a trooper. What do you think about taking the boys to Disneyworld? I think Joshua would love it."

I smiled and replied, "I think that's a great idea." I could tell that I had really touched Caitlin's heart by saying yes.

We stayed at one of Disney's properties after a friend, who had retired from Disney, gave us their friends and family deal. We were thrilled to have the full Disney getaway experience. On a beautiful March morning, we packed up the car and drove to Disney. When Joshua walked up to a thirty-foot-tall log cabin fort with a lookout, his excitement captivated my heart. Filled with joy, we climbed toward the lookout and waved at Caitlin and Ezra. It was another special family moment. And after a grueling last few months, this trip felt like it pulled us back together. These short vacations had become our family's lifeline, allowing us to get away from the stressors of life and bring the best versions of ourselves into the moment. I hadn't yet realized that this was an unhealthy cycle. As a couple, we didn't yet understand the importance of connecting with each other every day. And as the leader of our home, I was missing the mark by allowing work to determine how much I had left to give to my family at the end of the day. I thought achieving a healthy work-life balance was impossible, and the higher up I went in my career, the more this imbalance hurt my family.

Back at work, tension was mounting fast. I'd gotten exactly what I'd hoped for, and my influence and responsibilities were growing at GreenWave. I was now responsible for our suppliers, project schedules, and the financial model. And, once again, I was struggling to balance my duties as a husband, father, and executive. Overwhelmed with an avalanche of emotions, I sat down to write in my journal:

Jesus,

It feels like I'm on a roller coaster. My heart hurts with all that is going on and the fear of failure is consuming me. But I see now that it is just another thought and attack as the what-ifs pile up in my mind. I'm worried that we won't have the money to pay our suppliers; I'm worried about failing. Somehow this morning, I've lost my fearlessness. I feel so out of control when I'm not working. Please help me walk with You and handle this stress better.

This backbreaking tension kept bringing me to my knees over and over again as this endless cycle of anxiety and suffering kept washing over me. I was so hurt, and somehow I failed to see how far I'd come. I kept focusing on where things were *not* instead of dwelling on how far I'd come. Without even realizing it, I was allowing my mind to focus on the wrong things. Even though my heart longed to walk more closely with Jesus, I kept measuring my progress against our culture's standards instead of Jesus's standards. I was so afraid of failure that I wasted all my energy by focusing on the wrong thing—the problem. Amid the turmoil, I fell into the all too common trap of praying for the problem to go away instead of praying for my faith to grow to match the size of the problem.

Chapter 12

HEARING FROM JESUS

It was now early May 2018, and the national trade show came to Florida. This was GreenWave's target audience. For an entire week, the whole industry fit into a seven million square foot convention center. It was my first trade show, and each day was filled with back-to-back meetings that seemed to be miles apart from each other. At the end of what was supposed to be my last day at the conference, the inventor of GreenWave's technology pulled me aside with a request.

"David, I have a good friend from graduate school who mentioned that their marketing director would really like to have a conversation." I was exhausted but knew I couldn't say no. As a company, we weren't in a place to turn up our noses at any potential partnerships or investors. We were still years away from generating revenue and in need of a steady stream of investors to progress the company.

"Sure, just send me their booth number. I'll find some time to swing by tomorrow."

Having already arrived home late one night that week, I left a few minutes early to beat the traffic and spend time with my family.

"Wow! You're home early today," Caitlin smiled as I walked in the door.

"Yeah." I tried to smile back. "But I have to go back tomorrow for one more meeting."

"I'm sorry, David. That sucks. At least we can have dinner together tonight."

Caitlin was ever the optimist while I struggled to see the glass as half full. As I headed back to the conference the next day, I thought, *I can't believe I'm dragging myself all the way back out here for a single meeting.*

As I walked up to their booth in the south conference hall, I noticed its unconventional design. Shaped like a rectangle, the booth stood two stories high at a major intersection in the exhibit hall. It was draped in a beautiful clean white fabric, and the company's trademark blue was perfectly showcased throughout the space. Chris, the director of marketing, approached me with a smile and his hand extended. He was a fit, well-dressed guy in his mid-thirties. Like me, he held a high position for his age. I could feel a sense of comradery almost immediately.

As the conversation began, he burst with excitement. "It's so great to meet you. I've been keeping up with your announcements. We're really excited about what you're doing at GreenWave." I smiled and nodded as he continued. "One of my priorities here is to build strategic relationships with partners that are moving the needle on innovation. There's a lot of excitement on our side, and we might even be interested in investing."

"That's great to hear," I replied, blown away by what I was hearing. "We're looking for strategic partners to help us scale and cover some of the blind spots on our team. We could really benefit from your technical insight."

Chris nodded. The sense of mutual alignment was immediately clear, so I moved in for the close. "If you're open to it, I'd like to send over our deck and walk you through everything we're doing."

We shook hands and I headed back home.

Did I really just strike up a strategic partnership discussion with a major multinational? It felt great to be growing into a leader at GreenWave. Falling into old habits, my brain started spinning. If I were to raise this investment money by myself, I would be the hero, and my career would accelerate even faster. In the days that followed, the challenges of work mixed with my growth as an executive as I journaled:

Jesus,

My heart is both soaring and at the same time isn't as grateful as it should be to You. An undisputable theme is emerging in my life where I am called to this super challenging work, but You always give me favor and always give me protection to successfully weather the storm. So I just wanted to say thank You for hearing my plea and delivering me.

By late summer, Chris invited us to speak to his leadership team. I flew out with Ben and Phil. As we arrived at the company's beautiful campus, I took in the hundreds of acres covered in all types of different trees casting an arc of shade over meticulous modern buildings. It was impressive, and I tried to stay calm as I walked into what was clearly a big-time pitch. Phil warmed up the room with his perfectly honed humor and then Ben picked up without missing a beat, discussing GreenWave's strategy and the capabilities of our team. He closed with a request. "Seeing is believing. Come visit the plant and see what we're doing firsthand."

And with this epic close, we shook everyone's hands and headed home. Once back on the airplane, I quietly prayed that they would invest. I didn't notice that I was falling back into my old habit of praying for God to make things happen in my life rather than praying to become more like Jesus. Once again, my career aspirations consumed me despite my strong desire and conscious effort to walk more closely with Jesus.

In the days that followed, I was able to convince Ben and Phil that I should be promoted to the C-suite. Eventually, we agreed on the title of chief integration officer, signifying my role as the bridge between finance and operations. This promotion would mark an important step in my faith journey, as it would be the last time I would fight for what I thought was mine at GreenWave. What I thought was fair. I had yet to learn how to fully walk with open hands, but I was getting much closer to accepting the path Jesus had designed for me rather than fighting the world around me for what I thought I should have.

By October, Chris called and told me that they had gone back and forth internally but didn't have the support to make an investment at this time. I thanked Chris for the update, and we agreed to stay in touch. I started to realize how challenging and time-consuming fundraising was. By now, I was meeting with customers, suppliers, and investors on a daily basis. Almost overnight, my job had become a sales role. To our suppliers, I was selling them a vision of a partner who could change the industry. To prospective customers, I was selling them on a completely differentiated product. To our investors, I was selling them on a high rate of return on their investment. I believed in the company to the core of my being. I believed in our mission, I believed in the technology, and I believed in our team.

Pitch after pitch, we kept hearing no from potential investors. The optimism of the summer gave way to a sobering reality as the fourth quarter of 2018 came around. The bills from our suppliers were overdue. Our cash was drying up and it felt like failure was imminent. Fear kicked in. *There's no way we're going to make it out of this mess*, I worried. I had come from the corporate world, where paychecks were never at risk and the future was well-defined. *Start-ups are so different,* I lamented. *Hard work is not enough to succeed. What if we don't have what it takes to overcome these obstacles? How can I court investors when I have all these doubts?*

Yet as we got closer and closer to the end of 2018, our misses began to pile up. I tried to separate my accomplishments and identity from the company. *I've grown a lot in this role. I've learned a whole new set of skills that will serve me well in my next role. I could really do some great things at a company that had a better chance of succeeding.* I began to pour out my fears and anxiety into my journal:

Jesus,

So here I am. I'm trying to pick the pieces back up. This road hurts and I don't see any future at GreenWave. I don't know what to do. It can't be by coincidence that I can't see a foot in front of us. Oh, how my heart hurts and aches. Will You show up? Would You reveal Yourself and help me make sense of the noise? Will You give me resolve and strengthen me? Would You give me hope for the future?

After weeks of wrestling with the issue in my head, I prayed. "Jesus, I can't be the face of the company to so many different groups of people. I don't think I believe that we can do this anymore. I'm ready for You to take me to whatever is next."

> **Perserverance is like weight lifting—it hurts in the moment, but the result is strength for tomorrow.**

Up to this point in my life, I was in control of the direction of my life. I had unintentionally set a boundary on how far I was willing to let Jesus lead me. In an instant, Jesus was about to turn my world upside down. The correction from my prayer was almost immediate. I saw a picture in my mind, sitting on a throne casting judgement on the company. In that moment, I realized that the throne I was sitting on was Jesus's. In that moment, I was using my reasoning and logic to take control of my life. The picture Jesus gave me was like a whisper saying, "I see more than you do; you don't see the full picture. Will you trust Me?" Jesus was showing me a greater level of submission, even when it didn't make sense in the moment.

In the moments that followed my prayer, Caitlin, completely unaware that I was praying, walked from the kitchen up to our bedroom on the second floor. As she crossed the threshold of our bedroom door, she heard the words "the company is sold" in her heart. Relatively new to her walk with Jesus, Caitlin was caught off guard and immediately came to me. Confused by what she had heard, she hesitantly said, "David, I think I just heard from Jesus."

"What did you hear?"

"I heard, 'the company is sold,'" she replied.

Stunned, I tried to gain my composure as I began explaining to Caitlin what had just happened a few moments earlier. "I was just praying and telling Jesus that I didn't think we'd make it."

Caitlin, still in disbelief that it was possible for our two paths to be this interwoven, said, "This must just be a coincidence."

I spoke more fervently. "Caitlin, I don't think this is a coincidence. In the exact moment that I was thinking we would fail, you hear not only that we won't fail but that we'll reach the finish line. 'The company is sold' means that somehow, someway, this company will be valuable one day. This is a big deal."

As I began to reflect on those four words, a new thought emerged. *Wow. Jesus, with You all things are possible. A single word from You can reinterpret everything.* As the thought settled, a hunger began growing inside of me to hear Jesus's wisdom more often in my daily life.

> **It takes faith to believe that Jesus is at work right here and right now. Don't write it off as a coincidence.**

Over the next five years, there would be many critical moments in GreenWave's journey. Jesus would honor our marriage by speaking to me through Caitlin. What He would reveal to Caitlin would help me navigate the dark days that were to come. We were beginning to live our faith and walk in God's ways. It was the type of faith spoken of in Isaiah 30:21, "Whether you turn to the right or to the left your ears will hear a voice behind you saying, 'This is the way, walk in it.'"

My heart's true north was calibrating with the way of Jesus. I was beginning to understand what Paul meant when he said to the Philippians, "He who began a good work in you will carry it on to completion until the day of Christ Jesus."

Chapter 13

LEARNING HUMILITY AND REST

At the beginning of 2019, one of our strategic partners introduced me to a potential customer. I hopped on the call with their procurement manager, as I had now done more times than I could count. I walked through the slides with my usual passion and conviction, emphasizing the right points at the right time. As I concluded the presentation, the purchasing manager explained to me, "This is a really timely discussion. Our annual supplier summit is just around the corner in April. We'll be hosting it in Chicago. It's a great chance to get in front of leadership and present your story to them to get executive buy-in."

Before the procurement manager could get the words out of her mouth, I thought to myself: *That's what everyone says. Everyone is a "leader" today.* I politely thanked her and said, "It would be wonderful to attend. If you could send over the details, I'll review it with our broader leadership team and circle back with you in a few days." I figured this would be part of the sales process, and I was fine jumping through whatever hoop needed to be jumped through.

Over the next couple of days, I continued to look at their website and took stock of all the real leaders that I wouldn't meet at the summit. The CEO, the division presidents, the head of procurement, the head of research and development, and lastly the head of sustainability. In the days leading up to the event, I kept going back to their website to make sure my slides aligned to their strategic priorities.

The April summit was here before I knew it. Just a few days after this meeting, Caitlin and I would have a chance to get away to New York for some much-needed relaxation. As I walked through the turnstile automatic doors at the Hyatt Hotel in downtown Chicago, my nerves were relatively low. I'd given this presentation a hundred times before. My entire team viewed this as an ancillary task, so it was just me in the meeting. I checked in at the registration table and was escorted to the waiting area. As I expected, there were six active meeting rooms. If I was lucky, I might see the face of one of their leaders. I looked at the slew of teams waiting for their turn to present and chuckled to myself, thinking that I was just a small cog in a very large machine. As was now my custom before any presentation, I tried to center my breath to calm my nerves and recited a prayer that had become almost automatic. "Jesus, I give you this time. I ask that the words I speak would be from You and that I would be able to clearly articulate our story. Would You help me to honor You in this process?"

A few moments later, the procurement manager appeared and greeted me. She motioned for me to follow her to the conference room. As I walked toward the front of the room, I noticed that the room was much bigger than I'd expected. The tables were arranged in the shape of a U, and the company had five people sitting at each section of the table. I was outnumbered fifteen to one. This wasn't the meeting I had pictured in my head.

As I plugged in my computer, I also noticed that something else was off. The people in the room looked familiar. As my brain raced to connect the dots, my eyes caught the man sitting at the center of the table. I knew him. He was the CEO. Then, like a wave washing over me, I started to recognize the rest of the faces in the room based on the hours I had spent looking at their website. They were the division president, and the head of research and development, and the head of sustainability. This wasn't just a chance to present to leaders—this was their entire executive team.

My heart rate spiked, my cool and calm perspective gave way to the unexpected challenge of presenting to an entire executive team. All of whom were twenty-plus years my senior. I choked out the first words. "Good morning, all. I appreciate the privilege of being able to share what we're doing at GreenWave and how we might find a way to work together." As the first words got out, I took a few deep breaths and dove right into the story.

As the conversation flowed back and forth, it became clear that their team was becoming increasingly excited about how our two companies could work together. As I neared the end of the presentation, their CEO spoke up. "David, this is a really exciting topic for us. Historically, we haven't made equity investments into early-stage companies. However, as our focus on sourcing sustainable materials for products is rapidly increasing, I think an investment is merited."

I was floored. This meeting wasn't just about them becoming a potential customer; they were interested in being an investor. I had no idea that the words the CEO spoke would result in a new business unit being created within their company to be able to make this investment. As the meeting concluded, I thanked them for their time and dropped my business card off with each of the members of the team.

I had just delivered a big win. They were excited about being a customer *and* investing. This was a massive win for me personally and professionally. Yet in the aftermath of the meeting, something unexpected happened. My ego didn't soar; pride was nowhere to be found. Instead, I walked out of the conference room and prayed. "Only You, Jesus. Only You could bring something like this out of nothing. Who am I that You would treat me so kindly?" I was learning humility and to see Jesus's hand in my success. It was no longer about how much money I made or what my title was; it was about honoring Jesus in my daily interactions at work and home. This shift began to cultivate humility deep within my heart.

> **Humility allows us to praise God instead of exalting ourselves.**

In the weeks that followed, Chris's company would get a new CEO and their interest in investing in GreenWave would be renewed. Over the next few months, both companies invested millions of dollars and created the industry validation of our technology that would act as an accelerator for us. It was the silver bullet we were missing in our presentations. Cash would continue to be a challenge in the years ahead, but it felt like Jesus Himself was leading me each step of the way. It was exhilarating and it was intoxicating. Jesus had stepped into my story and turned my despair into joy.

For the first time in my marriage, I saw my wife as an integral part of my faith journey, and my eyes turned toward home. At the same time, I was trusting Jesus to lead even the smallest parts of my daily life. Work began to shift from a pursuit for personal success and significance into an act of worship as I continued to walk with Jesus. With this subtle shift, I became even more at risk of overworking. I hadn't developed a balanced perspective on what being whole looked like. Mistakenly, I thought that Jesus needed productivity from me. I didn't realize at the time that Jesus was more concerned about who I was becoming and less about what I was achieving. In the Kingdom of God, achievement flows out of who are and is a byproduct of intimacy with Him.

With the wind at my back, I arrived home with only a few days to get ready for a vacation with Caitlin. Everything was lining up perfectly to take the battle armor off and rest. So far, we had handled the bumps pretty well, and we were about to celebrate our six-year anniversary. If you include the three years we spent dating, we'd now been together for nine years. Caitlin was, little by little, reducing her hours at work, and we were both fighting to find a good balance. Yet despite our progress, we desperately needed a trip away to recharge. Both our parents graciously offered to watch Joshua, now three and a half, and Ezra, now one and a half, to make our extended vacation possible.

Both Caitlin and I were amateur European travelers. While past trips were filled to the brim with as many cities as we could fit in, something different had happened to us as we both began to follow Jesus more and more. We began to long for stillness. The hustle and bustle of sightseeing vacations wasn't what we were looking for now. We desired a slower pace. Without much detailed planning, we picked three cities in Switzerland.

Our first stop was the cozy town of Lucerne. As we exited the train, both Caitlin and I noticed something was very different. Caitlin gave me a glance, almost silently asking, "Did you feel the shift in the atmosphere?" Smiling, I nodded while managing our relatively light number of bags. It felt like even lugging our bags across the street would disrupt this beautiful rhythm of movement that we were experiencing. What surprised us the most was that among the effortless flow of pedestrians, bicycles, and cars, no one was in a hurry. The pace of life must have been half of what we were used to. Walking around Lucerne, we rediscovered each other and took in the slowness of this town's pace of life.

As we went into a "local" coffee shop—actually the iconic one with the two-tailed siren over the door—we realized that even the milk in our cappuccinos tasted better here. Each sip seemed to calm our hurried hearts. Caitlin and I settled in and began to reflect on our lives.

"I can't believe how good this feels to my soul," Caitlin said with a relaxed smile as she took a sip of her cappuccino. "I want to move here and raise our kids here. This place is an oasis."

I took another sip of my cappuccino and nodded. "I couldn't agree more. And this is just the start of the trip. What a gift!"

From a marriage standpoint, getting away allowed us to focus on each other's hearts without the distraction of the kids. But from a spiritual perspective, getting away allowed us to zoom out from the challenges of the day-to-day activities of life and examine our hearts and our lives, and look for areas where things might be out of alignment. We accidentally stumbled onto this profound truth: There is a difference between a vacation that looks great on Instagram and a vacation that strengthens the foundation of your marriage. As a couple, we had made tremendous progress from where we had started back in 2013. We were beginning the process of connecting to each other's hearts on a deeper level.

After two days in Lucerne, we left wishing that we could have spent the whole trip in that magical town. But we were heading to what I had hoped would be the best part of the trip. We were heading into the Alps. Lauterbrunnen is known for its seventy-plus waterfalls, and we were staying at a hotel in the foothills of the Alps. We had both agreed that we would slow down our pace of life even more and made space for each other and for stillness. Fortunately, the snow at the base of the mountain had all melted. Even though it was spring in Switzerland, it felt more like a Florida winter. Just a few thousand feet above the base of the mountain, snow was everywhere. We had the best room in the hotel and the view out of our room was picturesque. Fully present and undistracted, we explored the valleys, waterfalls, and foothills of mountain. We even hiked up the mountain until we hit snow. The hike was a mix of quiet forests coupled with small towns all the way up to the Jungfrau summit.

As we ventured out on our hike, eventually the dry ground turned into mushy snow. Typically renowned for its skiing, many towns were closed now that the ski season was over. Undeterred by most things being closed, I looked at Caitlin and said, "Want to see how far we can go?" She smiled and began to run up the snow. As I tried to keep up, I noticed that the playful banter of our dating days was coming back out.

We raced up the patches of ice and slush until the tightly packed snow turned into wet powder. The shift happened without me even noticing until I found myself a lot deeper and wetter in the snow than I had ever wanted. As I glanced at Caitlin, I could see that look in her eyes of "let's go back." The fearless adventuring spirit of her youth had given way to a more measured sense of adventure in motherhood. Both disappointed and not wanting to ruin the time in nature, I looked on my phone for the closest coffee shop. The last town was just half a mile back. And so, with our trek incomplete, we circled back down the mountain.

Even though I was dead set on accomplishing a real hike, I realized that the greater accomplishment was connecting with

Caitlin. I hadn't realized how much my work and travel schedule had worn her down. She just needed to be seen and cared for. This week away from the chaos had turned back the hands of time. We came home rested and restored. But something deeper had occurred on the trip. As a couple, we were beginning to integrate the spiritual practices of the Holy Scriptures. The trip itself was a break from all the doing and achieving that was required of us back home and marked an important turning point in our spiritual journey as a couple.

Chapter 14

EXPERIENCING THE LIVING GOD

Just a few days after we got back from Switzerland, I got another phone call from Pastor Mark. By now, I had been attending our Saturday morning groups for a few years, and he had become both a trusted friend and mentor. As I answered the call, Pastor Mark wasted no time.

"David, I'd really like you and Caitlin to consider coming to our church meeting tomorrow night. I have a friend who will be speaking, and I think it will really impact you and Caitlin."

"I can check with Caitlin and see if my parents are able to watch the kids," I replied. With two small children, it would be hard for us to find a sitter on a Sunday night with such short notice.

Mark, reading between the lines, closed the call by saying, "I know it's short notice, but I didn't want you to miss it."

Pastor Mark had never pushed for me or Caitlin to attend an event before, so I knew this was a meeting we shouldn't miss. I mentioned it to Caitlin and then phoned my parents.

The next day, Caitlin and I walked into a small meeting room with about forty members from our church sitting in a semicircle. Pastor Mark introduced the guest speaker, who was also a pastor.

"Hey, guys," Pastor Mark opened. "I've mentioned Michael's name a few times before. Over the last few years, I have gotten to know him and have been so encouraged by his prophetic gifting. I asked him to come today to talk to us."

Alarm bells went off in my head. *Prophetic gifting? Oh geez*, I thought. *I've heard all kinds of warnings about this kind of stuff before. I don't think I've ever heard of anyone accurately speaking on behalf of God in our day and age. We've never even met this guy. How could a stranger hear from God on our behalf in real time?*

But as Michael walked into the center of the room, he seemed normal. Wearing just a plain white T-shirt with simple clear-frame glasses, he began to talk about his background and how he had experienced this prophetic gifting in his own life.

"I can't really explain how the Lord speaks to me," he said. "One time, I was prophesying, and this guy was being disrespectful in the house of the Lord and the Lord showed me that he had a joint in his pocket. The Lord told me to confront him about his attitude. So I said 'Even now as you have this attitude, there is a joint in your left pocket. Take it out of your pocket.' The young man was shocked as he pulled the joint out of his jeans."

Michael told a few more stories, like one about getting the nine digits of a phone number to call with a specific message and another story about a New York cop who received guidance from the Holy Spirit in his quest to locate missing children. He seemed genuine, and I was intrigued. Michael's testimony of his life was reframing my thoughts about prophecy, but I was still skeptical.

Then our guest began to speak about our church. "I see a building with tiles that are multicolored," he said. He was describing the cafeteria where our church met, so we all looked over at Pastor Mark, thinking he'd told Michael about the cafeteria.

Aware of the glances, Mark chimed in. "I know, guys, but we've never talked about the school or the cafeteria."

I still wasn't convinced Michael was sharing insights that he'd learned before our gathering. But what he did next surprised even me. He asked the group if anyone would like prayer. One by one, members of our church approached him. The prayers were much more specific than anyone expected. Michael was prophesying with authority and passion over complete strangers.

After about the tenth prayer, I decided to see what he would speak over me. "Hi, I'm David."

Michael asked if he could put his hand on my shoulder and I nodded yes. "David, you have wisdom beyond your years and the gift of administration, like that of a CEO."

Not bad, I thought, *but it's still pretty generic*. I figured Pastor Mark had mentioned my profession in passing.

"I see five smooth stones. You only need one stone to slay the giant. Remember, David couldn't put on Saul's armor. It didn't fit him. Don't try to wear Saul's armor. You don't need it." Now he was speaking of deep things that were registering in my heart. Then he paused for a moment that felt like an eternity and concluded by saying, "And remember the Word of God is a light to your path. It's not an LED light."

Those final few words blew the door to my heart wide open. For the last few weeks, I had been lamenting in my journal about not being able to see which way to go. I wrote that I felt like I couldn't even see my hand in front of my face. I was in a wrestling match with God that I hadn't even shared with Caitlin. Michael's words felt like I was hearing directly from God. My paradigm was turned upside down. Michael went on to prophesy over Caitlin and spoke words that were etched into my heart. He called out her true identity and spoke life into places of hurt. I was in awe of how we experienced the heart of God through Michael.

On the drive back home, I replayed the evening over and over in my head. I kept coming back to one thing Michael had said during his introduction. "This gift I have is cultivated in silence." I longed to hear Jesus's voice for myself, but I never realized that by having every moment of my day filled with noise, Jesus would literally have to shout for me to hear Him. In that moment, I became aware of how little space I'd actually left in my day for Jesus to speak to me—and for me to listen.

> **Hearing from Jesus requires us to turn off the noise from the outside world.**

Chapter 15

HEARING FROM THE HOLY SPIRIT

As spring 2019 turned into summer, work reached maximum velocity. Our pilot plant was operational, and my role as chief integration officer put me in the center of almost every strategic initiative within the company. I was starting to travel much more frequently, and Caitlin was left handling everything at home with our young boys. Caitlin needed my support more than ever, but I missed her unspoken cry for help as the urgency at work continued to get the best of my attention, focus, and effort. As managing the family took a greater and greater toll on Caitlin, she continued to slowly reduce her hours at work in an effort to support the needs of our family. As she began to work less, I felt like I had delivered to her the American dream. I was finally able to provide for all the needs of our family. I felt like I had arrived. I felt like a hero.

However, under the surface, what Caitlin experienced wasn't provision but a robbing of her passion and identity. To Caitlin, I wasn't providing. I was sucking all of the oxygen out of the room. What I thought was provision, Caitlin experienced as loss.

It was amid this unspoken hurt that our family time was slowly eroding again, this time silently. I was trying to find just the right time to talk with Caitlin about another trip I had to take to our plant in Wisconsin. As I walked downstairs, I thought to myself, *This conversation is going to go badly. Just rip off the Band-Aid and get it over with.* So when I found Caitlin standing in our kitchen, I wasted no time.

"Hey, Caitlin," I jumped in. "It looks like there's another investor looking to visit the plant. I have a couple dates that could work for them and wanted to see what might work with your schedule."

"Again?" Caitlin sounded worn down. "You were just out there. It seems like you're taking more and more trips."

"I know," I replied empathetically. "I am doing my best to make these trips as short as I possibly can. I know that I'm putting you in a really tough position. I'm really sorry."

"I guess I could make Tuesday and Wednesday work during the second half of June," she said with a tone of resignation.

> **Without time set aside to slow down, you can very easily miss the warnings signs that you're offtrack.**

"Thank you," I replied with a sad, grateful smile. "I understand how much you have to carry on your own with the boys when I'm gone. I'm hoping the intensity will lighten soon."

"I know," Caitlin responded with a half smile. I could feel her disengaging as I made more and more withdrawals from her emotional bank account. At the time, both of us were unaware of the real toll the intensity of my work schedule was taking on our marriage.

Despite all the stress at home and work, my desire to chase the heart of Jesus had never been greater. My prayer all those years ago for a life filled with challenges to draw me closer to Jesus was being answered daily. A few days later, I was on my way to Wisconsin. I had settled into my own cathartic travel rhythm, opening my computer on the plane as it reached cruising altitude and working through my inbox for the first forty-five minutes. Then I'd close my computer and open my journal. After journaling for about thirty minutes, there was one final swap—my journal for Scripture. As the plane would begin its final descent into Wisconsin, I read a few chapters from the Bible to orient my heart for the day ahead.

I had my trips timed down to the minute, often arriving only thirty minutes before the investors. As I pulled up to GreenWave's pilot plant, which was the size of a small warehouse, I was reminded of just how far we had come as a company. Standing in front of the facility before the investor tour, I whispered, "Jesus, thank You for guiding us through the building of this facility. Would You be with us today as we meet with this investor?"

By now, every member of the team knew exactly what to say and when to say it during the investor's hour-long tour. My job was just to follow behind and answer any straggling questions. As the tour came to an end, I heard a whisper well up inside me: *Pray for protection of the plant.*

What a peculiar message, I thought. *Protection? We don't need protection. We just need the plant to run at capacity and finish raising this investment round.* But as everyone made their way to the door, this internal nudge wouldn't leave: *Pray for protection of the plant.*

I was trying to be more open to Jesus working through the Holy Spirit, so under protest, I dragged myself over to the far corner of our facility, where I put my hand on one of the foundational pieces of the steel structure. After a deep sigh, I prayed a quick and simple prayer that was barely audible. "Jesus, I ask that You protect this plant. Please send Your angels to protect each corner of our facility."

Well, I thought, *you're probably crazy, but at least no one noticed. No harm, no foul.* I walked away and raced back to the airport for my trip home. As the plane reached cruising altitude, I began to journal:

> Jesus,
>
> You prompted me to pray for the protection of our plant. I walked, touched it, and started to pray. But even as I prayed, my heart cried out for the plant to finish its ramp up. Please forgive me for my unwillingness to pray for what You put in my heart. Even though I prayed for protection, my prayer was so brief. Would You help me to be more willing and responsive when You speak?

The next day I got a call from Rob, GreenWave's chief operating officer. "Hey, man. I know we were really trying to get those samples out for your customers this week, but last night the plant was struck by lightning. One of our control panels was destroyed, but thankfully none of the plant's equipment was damaged. We'll lose a week or two getting a new control panel."

I hung up the phone and fell to my knees. First, I was stunned that the voice I'd heard the day before was actually the Holy Spirit, which I had doubted in that moment. Next, a wave of humility washed over me as I realized that I had been entrusted by God to pray for the protection of our plant. Finally, I was overcome with fear. I was so close to dismissing the Holy Spirit's gentle nudge. What if I had ignored it? *Jesus, only You could orchestrate protection over the plant like this. Who is like You? You are truly the living God.*

This simple but profound experience began to change me. I listened more closely and submitted more openly to the leading of the Holy Spirit. As a young man, I had thought following Jesus was about obeying a list of rules that made life boring—and I had resisted. But I was so wrong. Now, as an adult, I was beginning to understand that the Holy Scriptures aren't a list of rules to follow; they are a guide to show us how to experience the majesty of the Kingdom of God on this side of heaven. In the days that followed, I began to spend more time studying the Scriptures. I also began to notice that I was becoming less drawn to books on business and success. Instead, I found a hunger emerging inside of me to read books that helped me grow in my walk with Jesus. As I did, I watched my heart align more closely with God. Caitlin noticed a difference, too.

"Are you coming to bed?" she asked me one evening.

I looked up from my book. "Not right now. I think I'm going to stay up a bit longer and read."

"Another John Bevere book?" she asked inquisitively.

I smiled. "Yep! His writing is so profound. He's talking about idolatry and how we still worship idols today. It just looks a little different in our modern age. He says that idolatry is anything we value more than our relationship with God. Like work or football or money."

"Interesting," my wife continued. "I've noticed that you're waking up early to spend time with Jesus *and* you're staying up late for the same reason. You should be exhausted, but I've never seen you with more energy. I don't get it."

"I don't understand it, either." I laughed. "But I feel like I'm growing so much."

Caitlin said goodnight and walked upstairs to our bedroom. Two minutes later, she came back down. "David, I just heard the words 'He who sustains me' when I walked in our room. I think it was the Holy Spirit saying that your strength is coming from God."

"Wow. That is beautiful," I replied. I stood up and hugged Caitlin and, for an instant, time stood still as I felt seen and cared for by both Jesus and my wife. As she headed back to bed, I wiped the tears away from my eyes and thought: *Jesus, You're at work in our home, too. I'm in awe at how You're gently drawing Caitlin to You. You really are walking before me and standing behind me. I am so grateful.* Without even realizing it, my gratitude rolled into a prayer. "Jesus, I had no idea when You said that You came to give us an abundant life that this is what You meant. Thank You for always showing up for me and my family. Would You continue to transform my heart?"

Week after week, the presence of Jesus became more tangible in our lives. Both Caitlin and I were being drawn closer to the heart of Jesus and back to each other. But for months, we had been going back and forth about whether we should have another child. The topic was a bit of a hot button, so I was taken aback when Caitlin broached the subject on a much-needed date night at a local restaurant.

"David, I've been thinking. I really feel like we should have another baby. I have such fond memories of growing up as part of a family of five." Caitlin paused for a moment before revealing the other aspect of her true feelings. "I also really want a baby girl."

I shuddered at the thought of a third child given our current stress level—but I kept my composure. "I understand, but we're just now getting out of the baby stage. Aren't you enjoying it? I grew up with only one brother and it was great! Do you really want to go through another pregnancy, another recovery, and all those sleepless nights all over again?"

Caitlin responded with heartbreak in her eyes. "How could you look at our boys and not want more?"

"Yeah . . ." I smiled. "But we're barely able to juggle everything now," I continued, starting to feel anxious. "Why do you want to increase the difficulty?"

Dinner ended with a cordial stalemate. At the time, I didn't fully understand how strong Caitlin's desire to have a third child was. It was like a fire kindling in her bones. I was unaware of how deeply my hesitation was hurting her.

Then, in late July, even as we were still misaligned on the idea of a third child, Caitlin walked into my home office, confused. "I think I just heard the name Ruth."

I had spent my whole life being logical, but over the course of the last year, I had pushed myself to abandon what I believed to be the safe harbor of my own logic. I was beginning to embrace the unconventional guidance of the Holy Spirit that often had me walking down a road I wouldn't have chosen by myself. As soon as I heard the name Ruth leave Caitlin's lips, I lit up inside. *The Holy Spirit just spoke the name of our child!* I was filled with wonder and joy.

"Caitlin, it sounds like you just heard from the Holy Spirit."

Still not fully convinced, Caitlin tried rationalization. "No, I really don't think so. It was just a thought, right?"

"Well, when you said the name Ruth, it resonated fully in my heart. I was perfectly fine pushing back on a third child until I heard you say her name. There's no chance I'm going to fight both you and Jesus." I laughed. "I guess we'll be having a third child."

We hugged, but then Caitlin pulled away abruptly. "But what if our baby isn't a girl, David? Will you be mad?"

"Our third child will be a girl," I replied with complete confidence.

Caitlin persisted. "But seriously, David, what if the baby is not a girl?"

"Don't worry, Caitlin," I said, trying to comfort her but knowing in my heart that the Holy Spirit was preparing us. "Our third child will be a girl, and we'll call her Ruth."

In the days that followed, I went to Carter's and for the first time walked straight toward the newborn girls' section, where there was a long row of pink onesies. I picked out three. They would sit in our bedroom closet as a declaration and daily reminder that the Word of our God would come to pass. Two months later, Caitlin shared the incredible news with me that she was pregnant. Just nine weeks into Caitlin's pregnancy, the lab accidentally sent us the gender of our third child. As Caitlin was reading the results, she pulled me aside.

"David, it's a girl! I just can't believe it. We're going to have a girl." I smiled ear to ear, enjoying our front row seat to Jesus's perfectly curated adventure. I was learning to open my hands and let Jesus lead.

Even as Caitlin and I were celebrating the news of Ruth, work continued to accelerate. A few days after our visit to the OB-GYN, Ben called. "David, I received an invitation to speak on a panel at our associations annual conference in Naples. I'm unavailable—do you mind doing it?"

Grinning but also terrified, I said, "Wow, that's such an honor. Thank you for trusting me with this, Ben. I won't let you down."

"I know," my boss replied confidently before hanging up.

A few weeks later, I walked into a ballroom filled with leading executives from the industry. Most had twenty, thirty, or even forty years of experience while I had been working in the industry for less than three years. I was on a panel with two executives who had spent their entire careers in the industry. Fear and anxiety flooded my heart and mind as I pondered every possible mistake I could make. My nerves were getting the best of me, so I reminded myself that I knew how to handle this avalanche of emotions. I acknowledged my inadequacies and prayed to my God, who was more than enough. "Jesus, I'm scared I'll say something stupid. But I know You are with me. Please give me Your peace, which surpasses all understanding and guard my heart against this worry." As I finished praying, I reminded myself of something a friend had said to me just a few months earlier at church function: "Don't be afraid of the limelight." In that moment, those words washed over me and I realized that Jesus had prepared me for this very moment. I just had to trust Him and step out onto the stage.

> **Peace isn't the absense of fear; it's choosing to trust the faithfulness of Jesus, even when it hurts.**

As the moderator introduced me, I walked toward the stage, whispering one more short prayer, "Jesus, would you give me Your words that You want to speak to this group?" As I sat down on the stage, peace began to replace the fear and anxiety. The moderator continued. "Our next panelist is the chief integration officer at GreenWave and is responsible for the company's fundraising and project management initiatives. David, tell us what you think this ecosystem needs to thrive."

"Thank you." I launched in. "I'm excited to be here. As a self-admitted outsider to the industry, I'm encouraged by the collaboration and innovation that's occurring here today. What we're doing at GreenWave takes a village, and we've been so encouraged at how everyone has embraced us with open arms. Innovation on this scale is not without risk. We've been so encouraged by each one of our strategic partners who have come alongside us to share their expertise and insights. We're convinced that this support will help us anticipate tomorrow's challenges. They've helped us refine our product formulations, approach to safety, and our go-to-market strategy. I believe it is this type of collaboration that can transform our industry."

As I was speaking, I was taken aback at the poise under pressure I was showing. I was demonstrating an executive presence that I didn't know I had. Somehow that day, the Holy Spirit stepped into the gap and helped me articulate with passion and conviction a vision for the future that inspired and engaged the audience for the entire forty-five-minute length of the panel. Jesus was helping me face each challenge. In the days that followed conference, I would journal:

Jesus,

Against all odds, You have given me a family—at work, at church, and in my home. This is from a boy who always ran away when things got hard. You've kept me in the fight. You've given me the strength I've needed. I'm weary of all the work on my plate, but I know that You are in control. So, as I sit here in the quiet, I thank You for every word that You've spoken. You have been so faithful to me.

As 2019 came to a close, Caitlin and I found quiet moments together on the weekend. Despite all my travel, we were getting better at making it all work and watching our two boys grow closer. We were savoring the final months of being a family of four. The year ended with another seven-figure investment from a family office, giving GreenWave a much-needed infusion of cash. I had been instrumental in shepherding the investors through the process, and 2020 was shaping up to be the company's breakout year. After struggling for so long, we were finally on the precipice of scaling. It looked like we were ready to build our commercial facility. But then, out of nowhere, COVID hit like a perfectly timed blitz that no one saw coming.

Chapter 16

WHEN THE HOLY SPIRIT LEADS

As we rolled into 2020, GreenWave was on the precipice of closing its nine-figure commercial loan from Lincoln Bank to finance the construction of its commercial facility. In just a matter of weeks, we witnessed in disbelief as an unknown virus turned the world upside down. By March, COVID had become a global pandemic and was impacting every aspect of life, adding a brutal layer of complexity to our financing negotiations. To make matters worse, Caitlin and I noticed a major shift in our son Joshua's behavior. As his preschool classes moved online, Joshua's safety and structure was ripped out from under him. The abrupt social isolation brought on by COVID seemed to trigger something deep and troubling inside him. Unable to understand what was going on and too young to communicate his feelings and thoughts clearly,

Joshua began to struggle. He needed time with me but didn't know how to ask. I was missing all the warning signs as I tried to adjust to the pandemic. With my coping mechanisms frayed and stress mounting, I couldn't see how much Joshua needed his dad present. It was a perfect storm—and like so many around the world, we struggled to keep our family afloat in the rough seas.

Back at work, it felt like every time we were close to finally raising all the money we needed for the financing, something unexpected happened. It was a challenging roller-coaster ride every day—all in the middle of a pandemic and meltdowns at home. I remember the sinking feeling one morning when Ben called me to deliver more bad news.

"David, the latest investment firm seems to be another bust. Could you take a shot and see if you can salvage anything?"

Exhausted, and with both our founders striking out, I didn't hold much hope that I'd be able to add much value to the effort. Yet as I spoke to one of the firm's partners, I saw a chance to pull the deal together. My time working as a consultant had taught me how to bridge two sides of a negotiation, and I recognized an opportunity to give the investment firm what they needed while still making this important deal work for us. *This is a $20 million investment,* I thought. *I've never raised this much money before.* I tirelessly worked through fifteen different types of documents and answered every due diligence question imaginable. It was starting to look like life had been breathed back into this once dead deal.

After reviewing my latest set of documents, the principal called and said, "David, I think this works for us. We're good on our end."

I couldn't believe what I was hearing. I felt like David before King Saul in the Bible, when 1 Samuel 18:14 says: "In everything he did he had great success, because the Lord was with him."

I had just turned around the largest deal I'd ever worked on, and over the next few days, I poured out my gratitude in my journal. I was yet again in awe of the places Jesus was taking me. I was riding high. But a few days later, I had a vivid dream about a large bed sitting atop a steel cage and being circled by a small remote-controlled car. Startled by the bizarre symbols, I awoke to what felt like an immediate interpretation from the Holy Spirit. *Do not let the investor back in after they back out.*

I walked downstairs to try and process the meaning of the dream. "Jesus," I wrote. "I don't understand. Is this deal going to fall apart? We literally just agreed to it a few days ago. Why are You letting this happen?" In the moment, it was impossible for me to see that Jesus was trying to protect both me and GreenWave, just like He did during the lightning storm.

As I lamented, I begged Jesus to help me understand. And in a tender act of kindness, He revealed his why. I felt the words "this is sacred" bubble up from deep inside me. It was just three simple words, but they had a powerful effect on my heart. I began to remember each of the times that Jesus had guided my steps before. His words always came at just the right moment. I was beginning to trust Jesus, even when it didn't make sense. This new approach to handling pivotal decisions was moving me from an awkward trust fall to a bedrock of my belief. In the past, I had allowed myself to only believe what I could logically understand. I was learning to look for Jesus's direction and valued His insight more than what seemed right in my own eyes.

For the next two weeks, Lincoln Bank asked for more financial restrictions and commitments from us. It was becoming clear that we would have to say yes to just about every request they made to close the deal. I continued to relay the ever-changing financing terms with the principal from the investment firm.

Within just a few weeks of agreeing to the deal, I received a call from their principal on a rainy Thursday morning in March. I was not surprised by what I heard on the other end of the line.

"David, I just got off the phone with my partners. Lincoln Bank's terms are too onerous for us. We're not going to be able to continue."

And there it was, step one in the Holy Spirit's warning that the investor would back out. Prepared for this news, I calmly replied, "I completely understand. I really appreciate your willingness to work with us and wish you the best." Since the deal wasn't supposed to be signed or funded until the closing date, nothing more was needed than the phone call. However, given my foreboding dream, I followed up with an email, meticulously recapping our discussion and the firm's desire to not participate in the deal. This was an unheard of extra step that I never would have done if I hadn't received guidance from the Holy Spirit just two weeks earlier.

In the weeks that followed, our CFO found additional sources of capital that allowed us to proceed with the closing. As we began to prepare for closing the loan, the principal from the investment firm called me.

"Hey, David. Sounds like you've made great progress with Lincoln Bank. We're ready to come back in and fund the project."

Even though the Holy Spirit had told me this would happen, I was still taken aback. It was like I'd been given a precise road map. Without missing a beat, I smiled to myself and responded gently to the principal, "I'm so sorry, but we've already moved ahead and secured funding elsewhere."

The principal became agitated. "David, it was only because of us that you got this far. If you don't let us back into the deal, we'll have no choice but to sue you."

Surprised by his threat, I replied, "I understand. Please give me a few days. I'll share this with our team and get back to you."

I hung up the phone and called Ben and Phil. "Hey, guys, they're threatening to sue us if we don't let them back into the deal."

My baseline disposition was to always try to find a way to bridge the gap. It was what made me so effective in my current role. But with such a clear warning from the Holy Spirit, I knew I had to fight to keep the investment firm out of the deal. Luckily, I had meticulously documented my final exchange when they pulled out. To my surprise, Ben paused and asked for my counsel.

"What do you think we should do, David?"

Without hesitation, I gave him the guidance I'd received from the Holy Spirit. "Ben, there is absolutely no way we can let them back into this deal. If they backed out this early and want to sue us, what will happen when there is a real issue?"

Satisfied with my answer and probably a bit shocked by my extremely uncharacteristic bravado, Ben agreed. "Makes sense to me, David. Let them know."

I immediately called the firm's principal back and with complete confidence told him, "I appreciate you working with us over the last few months. However, when you decided to not move forward, we found a different funding source. I understand you must do whatever you think is necessary from a legal standpoint."

"Okay, thanks," the principal responded unemotionally and hung up. I allowed the silence of the moment to wash over me as I whispered to the Lord, "Wow. I can't believe how You are moving. Thank You." Despite the mention of a lawsuit, the principal never made good on his threat and we proceeded with preparing for closing.

Just as we were finalizing the financing deal with second investment firm, the final wave of requirements came in from

Lincoln Bank. It was a hard pill to swallow and it did not sit well with a number of our strategic partners. And on a Friday afternoon in April 2020, I joined what would quickly become an outright hostile call.

"Where's Ben?" the vice president at one of our key partners snapped. I explained that Ben had a conflict, and I'd provide a recap to Ben later that day.

"I've looked at the documents you want us to sign. Frankly, we're quite displeased with GreenWave's progress. In fact, we're so displeased that I've asked our legal counsel to join this call." I braced for impact but was completely shocked by our partner's next words.

"Not only will we not be signing this amendment, David, but it's our belief that you haven't met the terms outlined in our contract. Please convey to Ben that I'll be moving to terminate our agreement."

We were already navigating an impossible tightrope. We had over ten strategic partners on the sales and supply side, and we couldn't afford to lose a single one.

Alone on the phone with this key partner, I listened to our company's death pronouncement. As I sat absorbing the vice president's torrent of criticism, I frantically texted Ben. "You have to drop whatever you are doing and join this call immediately. They are going to terminate our agreement."

> **Don't be afraid of the giant you find in the valley; we serve a God that brings giants down.**

By the grace of God, Ben joined the call a few moments later. With a front row seat to what looked like an autopsy for GreenWave, I muted my phone as Ben took the reins. Now out of the firefight, my emotions welled up. Feelings of despair and exhaustion washed over me as I listened to these two men argue over the fate of our company. In the utter chaos of the moment and alone in my office, I began to pray out loud and sob before my God. "Jesus, You spoke over this company. You didn't bring us this far just to abandon us. I know that Your Word doesn't return void. I've seen it with my own eyes. You are always faithful to Your people."

As the argument continued, I let the tears flow. I listened to Ben as he tried to save the company we had all poured our hearts into for so many years. As their conversation neared toward its inevitable impasse, I pounded my desk and cried out, "My God! Turn Your eyes to us! Deliver us!"

As the call ended, everything felt hopeless. And yet, hope lingered in the atmosphere. The fear in my heart was slowly giving way to the slightest tinge of excitement to see how Jesus would move in this moment.

To my old self, it might have seemed like my prayers were met with silence. But I now understood that faith, as described in Hebrews 11:1, was about looking at the impossible situation in front of me and choosing to believe that all things are possible with Jesus. We just have to trust in His way and His timing. I was finally learning to trust Jesus on His terms.

"Father," I prayed quietly, tears streaming down my cheeks. "You have declared the company is sold. I've seen You lead us through much worse situations than this. I declare back to You what You've spoken to me. Give our team Your wisdom and favor. Accomplish Your purpose. Thank You for Your faithfulness."

That weekend, GreenWave's board worked around the clock to put together a formal response to our partner. We leveraged every relationship we had within the partner's organization to gain support—and eventually, we earned back our right to survive.

The partner came back to the table and ultimately decided to fully support us. But, despite this huge win, it would take five more backbreaking months of ups and downs to finally close our nine-figure commercial financing deal.

Against this backdrop of chaos at work, Ruth was born in the summer. Unlike the boys, her birth was seamless. She came out looking great and was never once in danger of being admitted to the NICU. Unfortunately, just like her brothers, she struggled to stay asleep during the night. To make matters worse, work was at a critical inflection point, and I took days off instead of weeks off to care for Ruth. Summer slipped into fall, and we finally completed negotiations with Lincoln Bank. Once this deal closed, GreenWave would be ready for its next milestone, going public. It would be another monumental effort for me and the team. Amid this unrelenting workload, a newborn, two very active boys, an overburdened wife, and a global pandemic, our whole family was in rough shape. Caitlin and I were struggling at every level—as a family, a couple, and as individuals. Week after week, I poured out the stress, hurt, and exhaustion in my journal. As I struggled to not fail at work, I failed to be the type of husband Caitlin needed. Even worse, I was starting to see my kids as a burden instead of precious gifts from God. Caitlin and my children needed me more than ever, and I wasn't there to support them. I continued to process these challenges in my journal:

> Jesus,
> Ruth is almost ten weeks old, and I think she's taking her first long nap. I'm so grateful that she slept through most of the night. There is so much mess ahead. I'm scared and tired. I want to walk this path You've called me to. I only ask for You to give me Your wisdom. I

want to see Your culture flow out across this organization. I long for GreenWave to be a beacon of light to this industry. That we would bring hope to this global challenge. So I pause and ask for You to continue to lead us. All I have is Yours. Give me Your strength to run this race; let it be pleasing to You.

We had just received the closing date for the commercial financing when Caitlin came over to me in the kitchen. "David, my parents can't fly because of COVID, and I'd really like for them to finally meet Ruth."

Trying to be as present as possible as my mind was spinning with work pressures, I smiled and nodded as Caitlin continued. "Do you think once the financing deal closes, we could rent an Airbnb in North Carolina so my parents could drive down and meet Ruth?"

I quickly worked through GreenWave's October and November calendar in my head. Convinced the dates would line up, I said, "That should work out. Let's do it."

Caitlin smiled. "I know this is a sacrifice with everything you have going on, but we're long overdue for a vacation."

I knew I had touched Caitlin's heart after asking so much of her for so long. Working ten-, twelve-, and fourteen-hour days, often six or seven days a week, definitely meant Caitlin and the kids weren't getting the best of me, and I was starting to be worse for the wear. A few days later, we booked the Airbnb and everything was set for our long-overdue vacation.

In the days that followed, the closing date for the deal was set for the first week of October 2020. This was amazing news. We had spent the last four years and tens of thousands of hours fighting to be able to satisfy every requirement to close on the deal. But as soon as I sighed in relief, Ben called me. "I just got off the phone with the bankers, David. They want us to put a lot more cash into the deal."

I gasped, struggling to find the words. "It's taken us years to get here. It takes months to raise that kind of money. This is absurd!"

"The bankers smell blood in the water," Ben commiserated, "and they're pressing their advantage. We only have two weeks to come up with the money. Circle back with our existing investors and see if anyone is willing to help us close the gap."

I shot into action with the rest of the team. We were able to create milestones with Lincoln Bank in which the additional money would be set aside in the reserve account. And our CFO pulled off the most amazing lightning-fast financing round from an investment fund that he worked with in the past. Our existing investors and one new investor came to the table, as well. All the investment documents had been signed, and each investor agreed to wire their money only after our newest investor came in. With everything lined up, the only thing left was the wires to come in.

Watching the wires hit was one of the most fun parts of my job. We had just moved banks and were using a new funding form that I created. In almost every circumstance, the wire hit the same or next day. For this important closing, with an abundance of caution, our international investor agreed to wire the money on Friday for our Wednesday closing. But as Friday evening came to a close, there was no wire. Monday arrived. No wire. Tuesday morning, I called our controller to check again. Still no wire. I was starting to panic.

On Tuesday evening, I called our controller again. "Any luck on the wire?"

"Not yet, David. We're really cutting it close."

"Yeah, I'm really starting to get worried. If this wire doesn't come through, the whole deal might fall apart."

"I'm glad I'm not in your shoes," the controller replied, shaking me to my core.

That afternoon, as the seven-figure wire sat somewhere between the banks in the deepest recesses of the international SWIFT banking network, I did the only thing I could do—I prayed and journaled. "Jesus," I prayed, "this is Your dream. I know that no mistake I make could derail that. Help me remember that You loved this company long before I did." As I sat down to journal, I could feel the fear and my anxiety taking hold.

> Jesus,
>
> My heart is a mess. If I made a terrible mistake with the routing details of the wire, then I am so sorry. I have fought for this company with every bone in my body. I know that You called me here. My heart is sick. Help me. Would You bring strength to the places of weakness in my heart and mind? I look at each wave of fear, anxiety, and uncertainty and am consumed. Help me to look past this moment to the end of the story. Your Word is true. The company is sold. The battle is won, and I have the privilege of watching Your word come to pass. Thank You.

Wednesday morning arrived. It was the equivalent of our Super Bowl for GreenWave. I woke up early and called our controller again at 8 a.m. "Did the wire hit?"

"No," he replied, dumbfounded.

I had only ninety minutes before I would have to call Ben and the bankers and let them know that something had gone terribly wrong. Maybe I had messed up. The deal was already held together by the thinnest of strings. I wasn't sure the bankers would stay in the deal if we missed this funding deadline.

At 9:02 a.m., I called our Controller again. "Do you mind looking one more time?"

"Sure, David." It seemed as if I was on the line for an eternity as he checked. "Wow. It just hit. The money is in."

"Thank you!" I said, jumping with excitement. I asked him to send me a screenshot and quickly began calling our other investors to let them know that we were ready for their wires now. One by one, the remaining wires came in.

By ten in the morning, all but the last wire had come in. But it was the largest, an eight-digit wire. The investors wanted confirmation that the deal was ready to close before wiring the money. Everyone who had an interest in the deal was on a fifteen-plus person conference call. This included a range of investors, four different law firms, and our team. The call, which was supposed to be a short "check the box" confirmation call, quickly morphed into a *Judge Judy* episode as four law firms battled over the final language of the financing documents. The call extended into the afternoon as everyone sat on an open conference line, coming in and out as the lawyers tried to handle the remaining issues. My phone was constantly ringing with anxious investors wondering why no announcement about the closing had been made. Something had to be done to bring the deal across the finish line. With an audience that was responsible for managing billions of dollars, I mustered up all the courage I had to speak.

"Guys, I think we all know the final steps that need to be completed by the end of the day. I'm worried that if we can't find an agreement here, we're going to lose the investment from our last investor. We are really close to finalizing all the documents.

Could we let the lawyers work this out offline and close the deal now?"

One by one, each participant agreed. Then, almost in slow motion, I heard the moderator of the call speak. "I'll be turning on the recording service to confirm the closing of this financing."

In the most professional and matter-of-fact voice, she spoke like she was speaking into a microphone. "I am confirming the closing of . . ."

As she spoke, I thought, *Oh my goodness, this is really happening! Thank You, Jesus! You're so faithful.*

The escrow agent began to rattle off the impressive twelve-digit alphanumeric code associated with our transaction, then asked our lead banker, "Can you confirm the deal is ready to be closed?"

She then asked each key stakeholder on the call the same question. I had fought for this moment with every fiber in my being, for years. I was overcome with awe as each participant replied yes.

After the final yes, the moderator paused and said: "This confirms the closing ..." The moderator went on to deliver the twelve-digit alphanumeric ISIN code and then immediately dropped the call. We had defied the odds and done the impossible. We had finally closed the financing. Like everyone else at GreenWave, I was ecstatic.

I ran downstairs to tell Caitlin. I was bursting with excitement as I ran over to her and shouted, "We did it, Caitlin! We closed on the financing! We can finally build our plant!" I was like a child celebrating their birthday.

"That's so great, David," Caitlin said with a half smile. "I'm really proud of you."

Thinking her tepid response meant she didn't fully understand my news, I tried harder to explain what had just happened.

"Caitlin, we finally closed on the deal, we just raised over one hundred million dollars—after all these years and hard work. I can't believe it."

Busy readying our family for the evening routines, she gave me a quick, exhausted hug. "I'm so happy for you, David."

I longed to celebrate this monumental accomplishment with her. She had sacrificed so much for us to get to this point, but she didn't see this accomplishment as her victory, too. I knew we were struggling, but it would take time for me to fully understand that this was a symptom of us walking alongside each other but not with each other. Juggling three children under the age of five with an absentee father had pushed Caitlin into survival mode—and I hadn't been helping her keep her head above water for several years now. I knew I had been called to support GreenWave's growth and mission, but I hadn't yet learned that you can be called to something without completely sacrificing your home life. Without noticing, I'd crossed a line. I thought I was providing for my family, but what they really needed was just me to be present in their everyday lives. As this epic day came to a close, I had one final thought: *At least we have our vacation coming up. This always gives us time to put the pieces back together.*

Chapter 17

A SHIFT OF THE HEART

After the financing had closed, there was no rest for the weary. It was time for GreenWave's road show to take the next step in our growth: becoming a publicly traded company. Thankfully, the road show would be virtual due to COVID, which meant less travel. But it was still going to be a significant responsibility on top of my already full plate. In preparation, I was promoted to chief commercial officer, a real C-suite title. The road show would be driven by our CEO, CFO, and me. We'd be asking for more than $200 million, so the stakes were extremely high and there was no way I could miss any of these meetings. Unfortunately, the start of the road show kept getting delayed. The second week of October quickly shifted to the third week until the unthinkable happened: The road show would now happen during our family trip.

Realizing that our desperately needed vacation was now threatened, I walked downstairs and found Caitlin in the kitchen making some snacks for the kids. "Hey, Caitlin, I have some really bad news. The road show has shifted back another week. It's now going to happen the same week as our vacation."

"What?" Caitlin swung around. "I can't see my parents? They can't meet Ruth? We've been quarantining for the last week just to make sure we can see them. This is our only chance!"

I felt physically sick as I shared the news. "I know." I apologized earnestly. "We can still go, but I'll be in back-to-back presentations from eight in the morning to five in the evening. I wish I could move the road show—I really do, but it's out of my control."

"Okay," Caitlin said quietly as she turned back to making snacks. I could tell she was upset but relieved that she could still see her parents and introduce them to our daughter, who was now almost four months old.

The next week, the five of us piled into our SUV and made the ten-plus-hour drive to North Carolina. It was taxing as I tried to wrap my head around the twenty-plus presentations ahead as Caitlin juggled our three young children who had never been stuck in a car for the entire day. After what felt like forever, we finally arrived at our oversize Airbnb just outside of Asheville. As we took our own self-guided tour of the home, I realized that we'd need to make some adjustments to our original plan. Instead of settling into the primary bedroom, we moved into a small room downstairs so we could sleep near our kids. Meanwhile, I canvased the house for a space that I could temporarily use for all my meetings. There wasn't a desk in the entire place and the open layout of the house meant that only the bedrooms offered privacy with a door. A sickening thought swept over me as I realized that the large dresser in our bedroom was the only viable option. I'd have to stand all day while I delivered my pitches.

After completing the first two days of pitches and feeling guilty about Caitlin juggling the kids and her parents alone, I curled up on our bed and journaled my frustration. I told Jesus that my desire was to honor Him but that I was breaking myself and my marriage in the process. On the third day, after I'd finished my morning pitches, Caitlin pulled me aside.

"David, I really need a break." I could hear the desperation and agitation in her voice. "If you could watch Ruth so I can take the boys out with my dad, I would really appreciate it." Caitlin had given so much and demanded so little—and her tone indicated that this was more than a request. I understood immediately what was needed.

"Absolutely," I said, fully understanding that this wasn't the vacation I'd promised her. But the idea of holding my four-month-old daughter while doing pitches to investors who I'd never met was beyond absurd. And while this wild turn of events completely surprised me, I knew that Jesus wasn't caught off guard by it. As I raced to gain control of my emotions, I prayed. "Jesus, I know You go before me. I know You're not surprised by this. You already know where the funding is going to come from; I trust You. Would You give me Your peace and the right words as I enter this moment?"

A couple of hours later, I was asking investors for hundreds of millions of dollars with Ruth perched on my shoulder. From a business point of view, it was the equivalent of trying to swim with concrete bricks tied to your feet. But I'd seen Jesus move mountains at every turn in this journey, and I was convinced that I was right where I needed to be. But I'd wildly overestimated how long Ruth would be happy with me holding her. She cooperated about half the time. An investor would ask a question, and she'd fuss. I would begin speaking, and she'd grunt or whine. I did my best to keep my composure, but my presentations did not go as smoothly as I'd hoped. Nothing went completely south, but I wasn't at my best. I was so happy when I finished my last presentation and could finally spend a few hours giving Caitlin and the kids my full attention.

Dinner was quiet and relaxing until my phone buzzed as we were finishing eating. I quickly silenced my phone, but within a few seconds, there were more vibrations. A quick glance revealed a group text between our CFO and a promising investor. "I'm looking through the pitch deck and have a few questions," the investor texted. "Do you have five to ten minutes this evening to run through them?"

I'd been raising money long enough to know this wasn't actually a question; it was a request and time was of the essence. On autopilot, I leaned over to Caitlin and whispered, "I need to reply to a potential investor who has a few questions. It should be a pretty quick call."

Caitlin nodded somberly, and I slipped back downstairs to take the call, which ended up being hours of due diligence as the investor grilled both me and our CFO. Finally, as the clock struck nearly midnight, the investor asked, "What else am I missing?"

Exhausted, I replied, "I think we've covered just about all of it."

I hung up and felt that same wave of shame and deep sadness that I'd felt when I'd missed my dad's birthday so many years earlier. The sense of guilt and regret was overwhelming. I thought to myself: *This time things were different. The stakes were much higher. I didn't have a choice. I was doing what my job required.* It only took a few seconds to realize that I was trying to rationalize my behavior.

As I crawled into bed, I whispered to Caitlin, "I'm so sorry. I had no idea it would take hours." There was no response.

> It is in the moment of confessing our failure that we invite the power of the Holy Spirit in to transform us.

When our family "vacation" came to a close, I realized this trip had been very different—in the worst sense of the word. On other vacations, I'd been fully present and delighted in spending time together. The memories of this vacation were of me sitting alone in the basement on investment calls while my wife missed the break she deserved. Vacations had always drawn us closer together as a couple, but this trip had pushed us further apart. I knew I'd gone too far this time. I'd lost my wife's heart and her trust. The tremendous toll my job was taking on my marriage and family was beginning to sink in—and the weight of it was crushing.

Arriving home more exhausted than we'd left, we fell back into our normal routines. Fortunately, the week of vacation that I sacrificed for our pitches had resulted in us raising enough money to take GreenWave public. Despite the progress at work, the tension between me and Caitlin was near an all-time high. A few weeks later, I learned my new annual salary would almost double with the potential for significant bonuses. In addition, my company stock now had the potential to create meaningful wealth for our family. And yet no amount of money in our bank account could heal the wounds that had fractured our relationship. Despite our challenges, tithing had become a foundational practice for us. After watching Jesus faithfully walk us through impossible odds, we found our hearts in a posture where we wanted to give more than a tithe. We wanted to live in alignment with Proverbs 3:9, which says, "Honor the Lord with your wealth, with the first fruits of all your increase." But we also knew there was something greater at work.

Jesus, in less than a decade, had taken me from a boy who'd spent every penny on himself—and Caitlin, who rolled her eyes at giving to the church—and opened our hearts to generosity. Just like Hebrews 11:34 declares, Jesus took our weakness and turned it into a strength. And yet there was another lesson hidden in our tithing. It was actually tithing that protected us from that awful treadmill of greed where you're never satisfied with what you have and always want more. We gave and, to my surprise, we found peace in our finances even though it meant that we couldn't get a yacht or a vacation home. We wanted to make sure we didn't think about the money as ours because our provision came from Jesus.

> **Our spiritual practices quietly compound over time; it can take years to see the fruit mature.**

With GreenWave finally on stable ground, I had time to breathe and take a moment to observe the world around me. The first thing that hit me hard was seeing just how much hurt and strain the last two years had put on me, Caitlin, and our marriage. The cost we'd paid to get to this point had been much greater than I'd realized. Even though we were making great steps in walking with Jesus, our journey through the valley had left us with deep wounds.

Amid the heartache, I came to the realization that I needed a safe place to process the range of emotions I was experiencing. In the days that followed, I made my first appointment with a therapist to help me look beyond the surface to the deep things that were going on in my heart. With my therapist, we began to look for the root causes that were resulting in this continual pattern of striving, fighting, heartbreak, and coping. I had to swim upstream to where the issues were emerging: my head. If I kept trying to fight the battles in my heart, I was destined to never get out of this spin cycle. I had to fortify my mind. As Paul said in Philippians 4:6–8:

> Do not be anxious about anything, but in every situation, by prayer and petition, with thanksgiving, present your requests to God. And the peace of God, which transcends all understanding, will guard your hearts and your minds in Christ Jesus.
>
> Finally, brothers and sisters, whatever is true, whatever is noble, whatever is right, whatever is pure, whatever is lovely, whatever is admirable—if anything is excellent or praiseworthy—think about such things.

I began to be curious about each thought that came into my mind. I welcomed the thoughts that felt clean and from God and challenged the thoughts that felt toxic and didn't align with God's Word. As I stepped into the epicenter of my mind and looked at all the thoughts racing around, I noticed three themes emerging.

First, every toxic thought that I didn't race to fight against eventually made it down into my heart. The effort to get that toxic thought out of my heart was ten times harder. Secondly, I started to notice that some of the thoughts weren't actually my thoughts. The enemy had pushed those thoughts to me, hoping that I would think about them and make them my thoughts. Sometimes the initial thought didn't even appear bad. Then a new thought would emerge a little bit more offtrack. By the time the third thought emerged, I looked around and thought to myself, *how in the world did I get sucked into thinking about this*? It was such a subtle trick of the enemy, but I was starting to become aware of it.

Lastly, and perhaps most importantly, I began to see that when I read my Bible, the words stayed in my head but never found their way to my heart. Over the years, I had allowed the world to shape me and in doing so, I created a highway between my head and my heart for toxic thoughts. In doing so, I forced the Word of God to travel through congested bumper-to-bumper traffic to get into my heart. To fix this, I had to shift my perspective on how and why I read my Bible. I had to stop thinking of my Bible as a good guide for life that I should understand academically. I had to start looking at my Bible as God's Living Word. This shift required me to elevate His Word above my personal opinions and biases, to stand uncontested as the single source of truth in my life.

I began to pause when I read passages that I didn't understand. I asked the Holy Spirit to reveal what I was missing. I researched and looked into the passages that caught my attention. Ever so slowly, a passion for God's word began to form in my heart until I got to the place that I could stand with King David in agreement when he said in Psalm 119:11: "I have hidden your word in my heart that I might not sin against you."

> **The uncontested thoughts we allow into our mind shape our heart.**

In the years to come, I would learn from books written by John Mark Comer that despite all my recent efforts to chase the heart of Jesus, I had been unintentionally, spiritually formed by my habits, the friends who spoke into my life, the stories I believed about myself, and my environment. This way of thinking and relating to life was what Paul called our old self. He explains this in greater detail in Ephesians 4:22–24:

> You were taught, with regard to your former way of life, to put off your old self, which is being corrupted by its deceitful desires; to be made new in the attitude of your minds; and to put on the new self, created to be like God in true righteousness and holiness.

It was through counseling that I began to see these broken pieces of my old self more clearly. I caught a glimpse of the wholeness that Jesus offered, and I began to see another definition of success emerge. In the quiet hours of the evening, I thought, *What if I viewed success not in terms of title, achievements, and wealth, but through the lens of loving my family well and letting the peace of Jesus guide me?*

As 2020 came to a close, I had a call with a financial analyst. At the end of the call, he made an offhanded comment. "David, I keep telling everyone, 'Don't let how young he looks distract you from the fact that he is sharp and knows his stuff.'"

I was flattered and thanked him for his kind words. Then a thought flashed across my mind. *You might be able to make the Forbes 40 Under 40 list. If you just work a little harder and start talking about the company a little more publicly, you could emerge as an industry leader.* But as soon as the thought crystallized in my mind, I heard, *But at what cost?* In that moment, I realized I had changed. I was starting to experience the promise of Micah 4:6: "And he will turn the hearts of fathers to their children."

Chapter 18

HOW ARE YOU NOT OKAY?

By the time that 2021 rolled around, Joshua's challenges had become significant. Ruth's arrival less than a year earlier had only added fuel to the fire. What once were short-lived tantrums of saying no and stomping his feet had turned into physical aggression. Even getting dressed in the mornings became a monumental effort. Every shirt and pair of shorts was too itchy, too tight, too loose, or too old to wear. Caitlin and I noticed that Joshua needed more and more time to shift between tasks and activities—and no matter how hard we tried, we couldn't seem to prepare him for the day's frequent transitions. Desperate to figure out how to help our son, Caitlin began reading every parenting book she could get her hands on. As Caitlin focused on caring for our family, I continued to focus on work. We were stuck in our roles as partners, still failing to understand the high call of Jesus to become one.

It was amid this frustrating family dynamic that the Securities and Exchange Commission approved GreenWave to become a public company. The executive team was invited by the New York Stock Exchange (NYSE) to ring the opening bell. But with COVID's social distancing requirements, only five of us could attend. I was thirty-six years old and about to participate in a revered professional ritual that only a select few leaders ever experience. The honor was not lost on me. On a cold winter morning in 2021, I emerged from my hotel and made the ten-block walk through the heart of New York City to the NYSE building. Like a scene from an end-of-times movie, the streets were completely empty due to COVID. I was used to massive urban congestion in the heart of Manhattan. Today I could put my arms out, close my eyes, and twirl around without hitting a single person. The quiet gave me time to think. As I walked, I realized just how unique and special this moment was. And in that moment, my mind drifted to all the moments of Jesus's faithfulness. In those quiet moments, I celebrated that faithfulness of my God and in praising Jesus, I left no room for pride in my own accomplishments to grow.

The NYSE event was going to be a thrill, but I no longer wanted to be like the wealthy businessmen I had admired in the movies I'd watched as a child. I just wanted to be a better husband to Caitlin and a better dad to my kids. I wanted to walk more closely with Jesus. As I reached the NYSE building, I was quickly shepherded through security. As I turned the corner, I was stunned to see GreenWave's logo and trademark colors everywhere I turned. As our party of five filled the room, we took in the moment. *Wow, Jesus,* I thought, *I never imagined this would be the outcome of all our efforts. Such suffering, such sacrifice. I am so grateful for how You led us through the valley. I am in awe of Your faithfulness.*

After years of relentless effort, we were center stage in the heart of the financial district. It was like a fairy tale. A few moments later, we were lined up in our positions and got the cue to start clapping as we rang the bell and opened the trading day. Confetti shot out from every direction as we basked in our company's success. Despite the mountaintop experience, the moment was bittersweet as I wrestled with the price I had paid to get to here.

Over the next six months, GreenWave's staff grew to meet the expanded needs of the mission. I gladly began yielding responsibilities in hopes of carving out a more balanced life. As a result, my influence at the company began to wane until I was just handling sales and our European strategic partners. I had wanted to spend more time with Caitlin and the kids, but I didn't anticipate how my loss of influence would negatively impact my self-worth and identity. When opportunities arose to further my influence in the organization, I would remind myself about the cost of saying yes. I began to utter phrases that would have been unthinkable in years past—things like "I don't have the bandwidth to take this on" and "Let's have the finance team take the first pass at this." Each time I said no, I experienced both the joy of walking in a new direction and the pain of loss as my influence at the company continued to diminish. I was no longer the person GreenWave had hired—and I was comfortable with this new reality. I had run my race and taken the company as far as I could. It was time to start letting go and put my home life back together again.

> There is a cost to saying no. It takes courage to trust Jesus in the tension.

While the challenges of raising Joshua had been simmering for the last eighteen months, I hadn't quite internalized how taxing the situation had been for Caitlin. It was only when I was on a business trip to Vermont that I saw the magnitude of the situation clearly. Caitlin sent a text message with no words, only a photo of Joshua's thirty by sixty-inch-wide dresser tipped over with the drawers spread across the floor. We had drilled it into the wall so it couldn't be accidentally tipped over. But in a moment of anger, our son had ripped the dresser from the wall and thrown it to the ground. As I drove to my customer's office for a strategic planning meeting with their leadership team, I started sobbing and couldn't stop. The brokenness of our family had been captured in that single, horrifying image Caitlin had texted me.

Jesus, I cried out silently, *how can I be called to GreenWave when my family is breaking in half?* The pain that had been building for quite a while exploded all at once like a volcano. In that moment, the focal point of my heart shifted from work to my family. It was time to give them the best of me, not the scraps left over after work. A few weeks later, Jesus revealed that my time at GreenWave was coming to an end.

It was in April 2022 when I gave my notice and began transitioning out of my remaining responsibilities. My departure would take almost six months and require one last trip to Europe, which would be hard to sell at home given the state of things.

"Caitlin, it looks like I have to make one more trip to Europe before I finish my time at GreenWave."

"Are you serious, David? How can they expect you to travel over there again when you gave your notice?"

"I know and I completely agree. But I want to finish strong. I'm sorry to ask, but I need your support this one last time."

"Well, at least it's the last trip," Caitlin replied reluctantly.

I would be gone for one week and have two important meetings with a three-day break in between. The first meeting was in Frankfurt, where I was able to leverage the trust I'd built with both GreenWave and a key customer in an effort to help both companies find a middle ground amid my departure. Throughout the four-hour meeting, I was surprised at how helpful I was in bringing the two companies together.

As soon as the meeting ended, I headed to the airport to catch my flight to Stockholm, Sweden. A few hours later, I checked into the Stallmästaregården hotel. It was here where I was able to enjoy a three-day break between meetings and had planned on being able to do some long hikes before my next meeting. Unfortunately, the long flight from the States had agitated my hip flexor, and I was starting to realize that hiking was off the table. In the absence of spending time in nature, I began to think, *I guess I should fast while I'm here*. Almost immediately, the word *feast* crossed my mind.

A strong sense began to form in my heart that I wasn't supposed to fast but feast. After a few more minutes of processing this impression, I was convinced that this word was from the Lord. I walked over to the hotel restaurant for dinner, and I was impressed by the wood beams on the ceiling and the brass light fixtures hanging over the plush, semicircle booths. As the sun set, candles were lit, and the room came alive with a luxurious ambiance. The waiter came over and spoke perfect English. "Welcome to the Stallmästaregården. Is this your first time here?"

"Yes," I said with a big smile.

"Well, you're in for a treat. You're sitting in one of the finest restaurants in Stockholm since the 1950s. Our food is so famous that the hotel was actually built around the restaurant."

Before the waiter could even get the words out, *Feast!* echoed across my mind. I quietly smiled as I thought, *Wow! What an incredible and unexpected gift*. As I enjoyed the welcoming ambiance, spectacular presentation, and delicious food, I thought about how I would spend my three days in this lovely hotel since I couldn't go hiking. As dinner ended, a new thought emerged. *I'm going to use this unexpected pocket of time to dive into the Holy Scriptures.* And that's exactly what I did. Two feasts. A feast for my body and a feast for my heart. As I stepped into this feast, I experienced the gentleness and mercy of my God. Even though I had fumbled my way through the last few years, getting so many things so wrong, Jesus met me where I was at. He didn't reject me for my mistakes but leaned in to encourage me, like a runner struggling halfway through a marathon.

I used my time in Stockholm to think, reflect, and pray as this monumental life transition lay ahead of me. For the next three days, I took my Bible everywhere and enjoyed my own miniature silent retreat. There was so much to explore in this beautiful city, but I just sat in the quiet of the hotel and allowed myself to detox from the hurry, stress, and anxiety. Between reading the Bible, journaling, and praying, I took short peaceful walks through the vast and serene Haga Park, with its rolling hills and beautiful trees. As I came back from my afternoon walk, I sat down in my room to journal before dinner.

Jesus,

I am in awe of how You have orchestrated this trip. I never would have thought that I would be able to get away like this. I realize that You are helping me unwind decades of wrong thinking. I want to be able to sustain Your presence. Would You take the heart of this boy and transform me into a man who is able to carry the weight of leading my family? As I look at all unknowns ahead of me in this next season, fear yet again consumes me. I feel like I'm not enough. But I feel like You're whispering "You don't have to be." Please help me to stop worrying about tomorrow. Help me to hand over weariness and anxiety.

A few days later, I was back at home and in the throes of dealing with house chores, kids yelling, and an exhausted wife. It was like an ocean tide washed away the fragile sandcastle of rest and peace I'd built in Stockholm. My anger, agitation, and frustration came flooding back amid the chaos. After yelling at one of our kids for not listening, Caitlin had had enough.

"David, you've been gone for eight days and enjoyed a three-day break in Stockholm. How are you not okay?"

As her frustration boiled over, I thought, *She's right! How in the world am I not okay? All I did in Sweden was read the Bible and pray. Why am I worse instead of better?*

> **Each time we begin a new spiritual practice, we sow seeds of faith. Don't be afraid if you go backward before you go forward.**

Unable to come up with a coherent response to my wife's legitimate question, I said, "You're right, Caitlin. I don't know why I'm not better. I'll try harder next time."

I could see her cringe. She didn't want me to try harder. She simply needed me to do better. The interaction struck a painful chord in my heart. I had three days of solitude in Sweden while she was at home holding down the fort yet again. I thought I was coming back refreshed, full, and ready to be the best husband and dad that I could be. But the reality was that I had underestimated how much I needed to grow to handle the day-to-day stressors of our life with ease. It would take me another two years to be able to answer my wife's question. The answer, in hindsight, was that this practice of silence, solitude, and spending time reading the Holy Scriptures was like sowing seeds into my heart. It would take almost two years of sowing these seeds before I began to see a gentler and kinder version of myself emerge. I was beginning to realize that spiritual transformation was more like a seed growing into a tree. As my time at GreenWave came to a close, I wrote in my journal:

Jesus,

It is such a gift that I don't know what is next. You have hidden it from me so that I can learn to be present in the moment. And yet I find my heart still mourning my departure at GreenWave. It's like I've lost part of myself. At each step along the way, I didn't fight You to stay. I have kept my hands open before You, even as You have taken things out. It feels like a retreat, but I know the truth. You called me to be a shepherd and entrusted me with this company. I declare before You today that I have stewarded GreenWave well and give back to You ten times what You put in my hand.

I can see how You were with me every step of the way. You told me when to turn right and when to turn left (Isaiah 30:21). Just like Isaiah prophesied. You used GreenWave to set me free from my workaholism that had ensnared me, and now You have turned my heart to my family (Malachi 4:5). As I enter into this next season, please help me to be more sensitive to the leading of Your spirit.

Chapter 19

THE DARK NIGHT OF THE SOUL

By October 2022, I had finally transitioned completely out of my position at GreenWave. We had been able to sell some of our stock, which allowed us to live comfortably and give generously beyond the tithe. As I walked into this new season, I caught myself thinking, *If I bring the same intensity and dedication from work to my family life, I should be able to win back Caitlin's heart in no time at all.* I went into this new season thinking it would be like a quick oil change. I had no idea it would be more like a complete engine overhaul.

I had arrived at this extraordinary moment in my life when I could quit my job at only thirty-seven years old. Jesus had faithfully shepherded me through all the ups and downs of the last season, and I was hopeful for what the future might hold. But nothing could have prepared me for the deafening silence of an empty calendar. For the first time in my life, my professional identity had been stripped away. I had no major meetings to prepare for, no strategic agreements to review, and no major decisions on the horizon.

As I began to settle into the rhythm of my new normal, I knew that if I did not choose my next step carefully, I was at risk of becoming the worst version of myself. I needed to do something productive. And yet in this new, unscheduled life, a subtle shift in heart posture began to form. I became less focused on what my next professional chapter would look like and leaned into gaining a deeper understanding of the Scriptures. I began to apply my fierce resolve toward inner wholeness instead of chasing the world's definition of success. I increased the frequency of my counseling sessions and began to read about the early church and its ancient spiritual practices—like sabbath (taking one day of rest each week), meditating on Scripture, sitting in silence, and praying in tongues.

By December 2022, Caitlin and I had begun marriage counseling—in addition to me seeing my own counselor. Caitlin and I had perfected the art of dividing and conquering, but we were like two trains running on parallel tracks that never intersected. In the first few months after leaving GreenWave, I found my efforts at reconciliation thwarted by Caitlin's busy schedule. I had woefully underestimated how long it would take to rebuild trust in our marriage. Caitlin had been in survival mode for years, and I was trying to insert myself back into her life and busy schedule. I was realizing that even after nine years of marriage, we had completely different perspectives on what a healthy marriage looked like. Caitlin thought that since we were generally pleasant to each other, nothing was wrong. I thought that since we weren't thriving, *everything* was wrong. We needed to find common ground but both stubbornly believed our individual versions of a healthy marriage were right. As weeks turned into months, our homelife didn't improve. In fact, me being home and not busy was disrupting Caitlin and the kid's routines—and my longing to repair our marriage only added to the chaos. I'd left my job to be with my family, but being at home was making things worse.

Not only was I *not* winning back Caitlin's heart, I was causing

> **God's dream of marriage is not that the other person will complete us, but that, amid the tension, we will both become more like Jesus.**

massive confusion for our son Joshua, who had answered to only one person while I was at work or traveling. Now I was part of the daily mix, with my own set of parenting rules and expectations. Conflicted by our different approaches, Joshua's frustration and aggression intensified. But now instead of directing it at Caitlin, he was directing it at me—and I wasn't yet prepared to handle it. Joshua's outbursts toward me triggered my past unhealed pain, which welled up like a volcano that continually exploded. I thought to myself, *I won't be treated like this in my own home!* My harsh and unfiltered reaction to my son and his struggles crushed Caitlin's heart—pushing us even further apart. Each night after everyone went to bed, I sat in silence before Jesus and reflected on the day. I looked at my poor responses to Joshua and confessed to Jesus how much I missed the mark. I knew that I could be a better father, but I didn't realize that my own personal childhood traumas were preventing me from being the dad Joshua needed. Night after night, I would ask Jesus to help me step up to the challenge.

And yet I had no idea I had found the key ingredients of breakthrough: persistence, brokenness, and His silence. Earlier in my life, I had always run away from or numbed out that horribly uncomfortable feeling of brokenness. I had no idea that brokenness is like jet fuel for spiritual transformation, and I had been wasting it. I thought that in His silence, Jesus was abandoning me. But the truth was that Jesus had never been closer; His silence was a gift because it allowed me to see the depth of my heart more clearly. Without realizing it, I was actually taking Jesus up on His offer to be persistent, which He spoke of in Matthew 7:7–8:

> Ask and it will be given to you; seek and you will find; knock and the door will be opened to you. For everyone who asks receives; the one who seeks finds; and to the one who knocks, the door will be opened.

Over time I began to realize that my reaction to Joshua wasn't actually about his behavior. It was a response to deep and unresolved wounds that I had from being bullied as a child. Each time Joshua had an outburst, it was like all my baggage would wash over me like a tidal wave. I was reacting to a lifetime of unresolved hurt instead of reacting to his tiny moment of disobedience. But things would get a lot worse before they got better.

> **Our brokenness is like jet fuel. We can either use it to catapult us into the presence of Jesus or waste it by numbing out.**

My brokenness only intensified as things continued to get worse at home. *This was supposed to be such a simple fix*, I thought. *How could things have really been this broken without me knowing?* Each day Caitlin and I were at odds as we disagreed about how best to parent our children. It seemed like every time I disciplined one of the kids, I did something that Caitlin disagreed with. The situation felt hopeless.

By spring 2023, we were at an all-time low as a couple and a family. It seemed as if there was nothing I could do to improve our situation. To make matters worse, we still couldn't sell our remaining stock and weren't sure when we'd be able to. In that moment, as every headwind came together, I felt like I was going full speed in reverse. As the turmoil reached maximum velocity, I was unable to sleep. But what felt like a curse was actually a precious gift from Jesus. In the dead of night, Jesus was creating space for me to contend for my family.

Amid those sleepless nights, I would sit on our couch in the living room and cry out to Jesus. At first, I begged Him to make the pain go away. I was like a patient yelling at the doctor to stop pulling the broken glass out of an open wound. I'd cry out, "Can't You see that we're falling apart? Each day we're getting worse! Where are You? You were so faithful at GreenWave; how can You be so silent now?" Night after night, I sat in the stillness and lamented, begging Jesus to make the pain stop—but nothing changed. Weeks of despair turned into months. The silence was deafening. Yet it would be through the silence that Jesus would bring forth transformation to me and my family. From the outside, it felt like failure was all around. But this was the exact process needed to bring healing and victory. It was so counterintuitive that it didn't even hit my radar.

As spring turned into summer, I knew that we needed to find a way to reduce how much cash we were losing each month. I began looking for something both professionally and financially meaningful, but my top priority was making sure that I still had plenty of time each day to prioritize Caitlin and the family. I spoke with Ben about the possibility of rejoining Adaptive Technologies, but the roles available at the time weren't a fit for my passion or skill set.

In the weeks that followed, I started helping a local angel investment group and a sustainability start-up. They were both working through challenges that excited me, so I leaned in and did some part-time pro bono work for them. By the end of the summer, both the angel investment group and sustainability start-up had asked me to continue my support more formally, so I formed my own company. These two organizations became my first paying clients. With a strong pipeline of prospective clients on the horizon, I was beginning to think that I had found my sweet spot. I was providing value to my clients, getting paid well for my time, enjoying the work, and able to fit everything into a six-hour workday with plenty of time for my family.

Even as I was finding some professional direction, I had still not won back Caitlin's heart. I continued my nightly lament, and God continued to meet my cries with silence. Ever so slowly, I began to realize that God's silence didn't mean He was absent. Like a good friend who listens quietly, my God was healing me through His silence. It was in the silence of my ongoing lament that I realized Jesus was calling me to rest, just as He says in Matthew 11:28–30: "Come to me, all you who are weary and burdened, and I will give you rest. Take my yoke upon you and learn from me, for I am gentle and humble in heart, and you will find rest for your souls. For my yoke is easy and my burden is light."

As I continued to pour out my hurt, I began to lay down my preference and thinking of how

> **Lamenting is a powerful spiritual practice where we pour out our hurt before God and then declare His faithfulness.**

things should go. I had thought that since I had honored Jesus at GreenWave and tithed, he would bless me in my career and financially. But the gift that Jesus had for me was the gift of becoming more like Him. He was renovating my heart and cutting out every piece of flawed thinking, generational hurt, and brokenness. He was teaching me how to yield my preferences to His way.

By fall 2023, my responses to Joshua were becoming gentler—though he was still struggling more than ever as second grade began. He was challenged in new ways and began to struggle even more. He fought us at bedtime, refused to wake up in the morning, and cried almost every day when we dropped him off at school. Joshua was getting so worked up about school that Caitlin and I were pursuing every possible option we had, from doctors to psychiatrists to therapists to even alternative medicine. We were willing to try almost anything to help our son overcome the extreme duress he faced every day. Amid this chaos, I was trying to build my company into an early-stage consulting firm. And yet what started off as a promising next chapter of my professional life began to fizzle before my eyes as the start-ups I was best suited to help couldn't afford to pay me.

As the momentum of my new business slowed, the bottom fell out. I could remember each time when Jesus had showed up before, but somehow this challenge was working my faith muscle in a way that I'd never moved it before. My heart grew faint as hopelessness took hold. I mustered the little strength I had left and prayed. Sitting in the silence, a terrifying thought crossed my mind, *What if this doesn't get better?* I had blessed the name of my God when things worked out for my good. But what about trusting my God when He didn't do what I was expecting? Could I bless His name from the depth of valley? I began to be reminded of the heroes of our faith that also went through these prolonged valleys. Moses in the wilderness. Joseph in prison. David hiding for his life in the mountains. Jesus in the wilderness. Paul in Tarsus. An insurgent-like resolve began to come over me and displace my pain. I was reminded of the words that Job said to his friends in Job 13:15: "Though he slay me, yet I will hope in Him." I began to realize that the only way through this valley was through surrender. I prayed. "Jesus, this trial is so much different and harder than anything that I've experienced. Would You give me Your strength to surrender my preference and let You lead?" Week after week, I surrendered, stumbled, brushed off the dust, and surrendered again. I was learning to surrender even when the outcome and results looked, at least from the outside, like there was no way that this could be for my good.

It wasn't until a few months later that I realized my faith had been tested unlike anything I had ever experienced. Amid this profound and impenetrable wall of brokenness, I realized that each time I poured out my hurt before the Lord and sat in His healing silence, I removed a brick from the wall. Day after day this simple act of faith dismantled the wall in front of me. My circumstances hadn't changed, but I was different.

It had been almost two years since I'd stopped working at GreenWave. What I thought would be a short transitional season had become a long and formational one. I began to be okay with the volatility of revenue coming into my consulting practice and started thanking Jesus for today's provision. Caitlin and I began to rebuild our trust.

As we neared the end of 2024, Joshua had completed his applied behavior analysis (ABA) therapy, and we were seeing great improvement in his coping skills. We also started taking him to a specialty chiropractor who was able to help kids like Joshua. In the months that followed, we added a family therapist into the mix to help him work through his big feelings. We even started a cub scout pack with our neighbors to teach him additional life skills and model how to work in a collaborative environment. By the power of the Holy Spirit, I was now able to sit in Joshua's tough moments and let his words and actions flow through me without being triggered. Like the grace my father had shown me when I'd blown up at him during my brother's wedding, I was now capable of giving my son the grace he needed to work through his emotions.

Through it all, I had prayed and prayed for Jesus to airlift me out of the valley, to take away my suffering. But in His kindness, He had a different plan. He was showing me how to use the spiritual practices that I had developed over the years—praying, reflecting, journaling, lamenting, and tithing to the become the man He created me to be. He had called me to trust Him and walk through the valley with Him—not to escape the valley altogether. He was allowing me to choose how much I would trust Him in the valley. Ezekiel 47:3–5 speaks of this mystery of surrender when he says:

> As the man went eastward with a measuring line in his hand, he measured off a thousand cubits and then led me through water that was ankle-deep.
>
> He measured off another thousand cubits and led me through water that was knee-deep.
>
> He measured off another thousand and led me through water that was up to the waist.
>
> He measured off another thousand, but now it was a river that I could not cross, because the water had risen and was deep enough to swim in—a river that no one could cross.

This is the choice God lays before us in each moment of our lives. How much are we willing to surrender our control and let Jesus lead us as King? For some, it is only to the ankle. For others it is only to the waist. But Jesus longs for us to fully surrender and let Him lead our lives. But even when we forget this truth, or waiver in our faith, or make poor decisions, God does not turn away from us or give up on us. He pursues us. He waits for us. He is patient and long-suffering that we might one day experience the fullness and extravagance of His love.

As I look back at this time in my life, I realize that when I tried to do things my way, I experienced fear and anxiety. However, when I trusted Jesus, I was able to find peace, even in the depths of the valley. The same peace that Pastor Mark had when his house burned down in Tennessee. Back then, so many years earlier, I'd been baffled by my pastor's acceptance of his tough situation and so mad at God for allowing such a bad thing to happen. Now I was learning to live it out my faith, just like Pastor Mark. I once again remembered Jesus's words in Mark 8:36: "For what does it profit a man to gain the whole world and forfeit his soul?" I realized that *this* was what was happening but in reverse. I had left everything I thought defined success—the career, the accolades, the impressive salary, the fancy titles, and the influence—behind, and in doing so, I had learned how to take back my heart.

> **It is in the valley where surrender does the deepest work in our hearts.**

My time in the valley wasn't wasted. It was shaping me into a man I never knew I could become. I was beginning to see these valleys as a gift even though they hurt beyond words. I prayed for strength and perseverance. I asked my God to bring to completion the work He had started. In doing so, I was praying the same words in Philippians 1:6, the words that Paul spoke over the Philippian church while he was in prison: "Being confident of this, that he who began a good work in you will carry it on to completion until the day of Christ Jesus."

As the months went on, I noticed a shift in Caitlin. As we worked together to help Joshua grow, she was experiencing a change, as well. Caitlin had read countless books, was attending a women's group, and had taken numerous parenting courses in an attempt to help Joshua. All her research, networking, personal growth, parental discipline, and hard work had led her to a revelation.

"David," she said one night after putting the kids to bed, "we have been working so hard to help Joshua develop the skills he needs to handle life's challenges. I feel this fire deep inside me to help other kids like Joshua—and other families like ours." She took a deep breath. "I think the Holy Spirit is leading me to quit being a Physician Assistant and become a family counselor."

I smiled and looked into my wife's eyes. "Only in God's Kingdom does He use all of our broken pieces to make a beautiful tapestry. I can't say I'm surprised, I—"

Before I could continue, Caitlin began rattling off all the reasons why her dream wasn't going to work: She was too established in her current career. School would require her to miss a few nights each week with the kids. It would cost too much money. And so forth. It would mean continuing to live off our savings for much longer than we'd planned. But as the discussion continued, I was reminded of Hebrews 11:34 when God reminds his people that He is a God who "turns weakness into strength." Jesus was calling her to help other families.

All this time, I quietly said to God in the middle of my conversation with Caitlin, *You were teaching me how to be a husband, a father, and a man after Your heart. This season of our lives wasn't about me launching a new career but about healing our family and empowering*

Caitlin so she could be a blessing to other families in need. We had come full circle. It was now my turn to support Caitlin. Just weeks before the deadline for the fall 2025 semester, Caitlin submitted her application. Unbeknownst to us, this counseling program was one of the top rated programs in the entire country. Caitlin was selected for an in-person interview and three weeks later found out that she was accepted into the program. She was thrilled and I was so proud of her. I was learning how to be okay without controlling the plan. After years in the driver seat, I was finally comfortable letting Jesus lead our family.

Chapter 20

HIKING THE SUMMIT

It had now been nine years since I started journaling, three years since I had begun to hold the Holy Scriptures in the depth of my heart, over two years since I'd left GreenWave, and two months since Caitlin had gone back to school. Over the last few years, I had taken two backpacking trips into the forests of North Carolina. These solo backpacking trips became a way for me to surrender the comforts of life—no running water, air conditioning, comfy beds, and so on—and put my life completely in God's hands. Each time I stepped into the forest with my red sixty-five-liter Gregory backpack, I stepped out of my small world with all its pressing cares and put my life in perspective to the vastness of God's creation. In the stillness of the forest, with not a single person around for miles, I could begin the slow process of exchanging the stressors of life for the peace of Jesus.

In February 2025, I woke up to the words, *Come to me in the mountains in March*. I mentioned this to Caitlin.

"I think I just heard from the Holy Spirit, Caitlin."

"Oh—what did you hear?" she asked.

"I heard, 'Come to me in the mountains in March,'" I replied. "Are you okay if I take a backpacking trip then, Caitlin?"

Flustered because of her relentless schoolwork, she barely glanced my way when she replied, "I don't think that will work, David. Things are just too busy right now."

Instead of arguing with her, as I might have in the past, I simply replied, "I understand. I'm just passing along what I think I might have heard from the Holy Spirit. If it doesn't resonate in your heart, then it wasn't from the Holy Spirit." I was proud of my measured response. As I walked away peacefully, I prayed. "Jesus, I asked. I give this trip to You. If I'm supposed to go, please change her heart."

In the hours that followed, Caitlin's heart softened, and she told me that she'd found a few days in March during both her and the kid's spring break when I could get away with minimal disruption to our family's meticulously planned schedule. I gave her a hug and thanked her for making room for this trip to work.

After two taxing trips into the Carolinas, I decided to venture out west to hike Mount Zion in Utah. My heart was captivated by the names of the peaks. There were three peaks called the Three Patriarchs, referring to Abraham, Isaac, and Jacob. The most infamous peak was called Angels Landing, and another mountain was called the Watchman, which echoes the words spoken in Ezekiel 3:17: "You called me to these mountains, I thought, and they echo Your name." That night I journaled to set expectations for myself. "Remember, these trips are about digging the well. You might not see the result of this trip for years to come, and that's okay. Be patient with yourself. Rain is beautiful, but it's the well you dig to capture the rain that ultimately sustains you."

I was maturing in my walk with Jesus and no longer looking for quick fixes to make things better. I was looking at each step, no matter how seemingly small, as meaningful and powerful. I was practicing both humility and patience, and becoming comfortable with the pace of Jesus, which wasn't always the rapid-fire, results-oriented timeline I'd practiced in business. Heaven's timeline was different, and I was learning to sit in the tension. A few weeks before my trip to the mountains, I came up with a plan to start my hike in the Wildcat Canyon and work my way down to the West Rim. It would be twenty miles of hiking downhill with one night in the wilderness. This route was a big shift for me. Ever since my first hike, I had looked for the most challenging hikes in terms of maximum distance and elevation gain. These hikes had a way of depleting me down to zero, which somehow got all the junk out of my heart so that I could be filled back up. It was like I was walking around with a dirty glass of water, and the hike allowed me to pour out all the dirty water and fill my cup back up with clean water. However, something was different on this trip. I didn't need to clean out everything in my heart; I just wanted to sit before the Lord. I thought this downhill hike better matched the posture of my heart and would create the right space where I could be more aware of the Lord's presence.

Two months later, I was on my way to Zion. As my plane landed at the St. George airport in Utah, I looked at my watch, realizing that I was actually running ahead of schedule. *I really thought I had no chance of being able to check in today,* I thought. *What an unexpected treat.* Within an hour, I was walking up to the information desk at Zion National Park. The young, serious female ranger asked, "Do you have a reservation?"

"Yes. I'm planning to hike tomorrow and Saturday."

"What trail and campsite are you hiking, sir?"

"Ummm . . ." I fumbled for my phone, unable to recall the information. "Could you look it up by my last name?"

Within a few seconds she was able to pull up my reservation, but I could sense her growing skepticism. It was clear that she was concerned about my ability to navigate the trail I had selected. "It looks like you submitted for a permit to hike Wildcat Canyon and the West Rim. That whole area is closed due to last week's snowstorm. I could put you at campsite number 2, instead, but it's a grueling hike with a thirty-three-hundred-foot elevation gain over seven miles—and there's still a lot of snow still on the ground."

Her expression of concern was now heightened, and my heart sank. That elevation gain was at the upper limit of my backpacking capabilities. Even worse, I packed my heaviest gear thinking I would be hiking downhill. My pack weighed more than forty pounds. As my perfectly planned trip took a hard pivot, I wondered, *Jesus, where are You moving? Please help me keep my heart open to this shift. I know You go before me. I trust You.*

"I just had some backpackers come back earlier today," the ranger continued. "They said that the second half of the hike was mostly through snow and ice." She paused, genuinely concerned about my preparedness. "Do you have any traction gear for snow and ice?"

"No," I replied. "I've only backpacked in the Carolinas. This is my first trip out west."

Now she was *really* worried. "We sell Yaktrax here in the visitor center. I strongly recommend you make a purchase." The ranger finished updating my reservation and handed me the permit with a cautious half smile.

All I had to do was sign, though her expression indicated that might not be a good idea. "By signing here, sir, you acknowledge that you will experience freezing temperatures at the summit and encounter both snow and ice. Remember your campsite is to the left of the trail."

Jesus, I silently prayed, *I'm checking my safety at the door. You know my heart. You know my intentions. I am in Your hands. Please protect me.* I thanked the ranger and headed back to the car.

The next morning, I arrived at the park at 6:50 a.m. hoping to catch the first shuttle. It was pitch-black outside and as I walked away from my car, I slowed my breathing to quell a sudden wave of fear. *Where is this anxiety coming from?* I wondered. I quickly ran through everything I'd packed to make sure nothing was missing. *David, you're fine,* I comforted myself. *You're just afraid of the unknown. Push past the fear.* Recognizing that fear was knocking at the door, I prayed silently: *Jesus, You called me out to the mountains in March. I lay this fear at Your feet. Would You give me courage?* I continued to walk toward the bus pickup area. With each step toward the bus stop, the fear that so intensely gripped my heart a few moments ago began to lessen.

By the time I made it to the bus loading area, there were already thirty people in line, which comforted me even more. Five minutes later, the bus departed, and we quietly headed into the darkness of the mountain. As we climbed the narrow and winding roads up and up, the wind gently tossed the bus back and forth like a boat at sea. When we arrived at our stop about twenty minutes later, the sun was starting to rise and the large group headed for the trail. It was clear from the water bottles and tiny backpacks that the rest of the group was not backpacking like I was. It was beginning to look like I was going to be the only one spending the night on the mountain. Our group slowly made their way up the switchback trail, zigging and zagging every few hundred feet as we ascended the steep slope. The forty extra pounds in my backpack made it nearly impossible to keep pace with the group. It wasn't long until I was at the back of the pack. As we approached the second mile of the trail, I noticed that almost all of the hikers had turned right toward the popular Angels Landing summit while I turned left onto an almost completely empty trail toward a much higher summit. I chuckled to myself as I thought, *Now you're at home, David. You're always on the road less traveled.* I took a deep breath, said another prayer, and continued my ascent. I tried not to push myself too hard. I could tell that my body was still acclimating to the 4,200-foot elevation. Every mile up the mountain came with about five hundred feet of elevation gain. This was the equivalent of walking up a fifty-story building every hour for six hours with an extra forty pounds on your back.

As I began to enjoy the solitude of hiking alone, I felt my body begin to find its rhythm. *Remember,* I told myself, *you're planting seeds of faith. The victory is in the rhythm and practice. You don't need a burning bush moment to make the trip worth it.* After climbing uphill for only a few minutes, two boys in their early twenties hiked up alongside me with no gear.

"It's a beautiful day," I said, breaking the silence. "Where are you guys from?"

"We're from Canada," one of the boys responded, "but we flew into Vegas a few days ago and decided to hike through a couple of parks here."

"You flew into Vegas and came straight here?" I asked with surprise in my voice.

"Yeah, we weren't fans of Las Vegas," the second boy chimed in. "We'd rather be in nature."

Almost as soon as we started talking, the snow and ice that the ranger had warned me about came upon us. "So what do you guys do?"

"I'm a consultant," the first young man replied.

"And I'm a banker," the second said. "What about you?"

"Right now, I run my own boutique consulting firm that helps early-stage companies scale. I started it after being part of a team that took our last company public."

The boys' jaws dropped. They explained their interest in the start-up world and how they both wanted to be entrepreneurs. They couldn't believe the serendipity of meeting me on a mountain trail in Utah. Really, what were the odds? I began to see where Jesus was leading.

I told them the GreenWave story while we walked—about all the fundraising, the roadblocks and challenges, the financing deal, and going public. Throughout our ascent, I kept asking the Holy Spirit, *What do You want to say to these boys? I see their hunger; how do I show them Jesus clearly?*

After an hour of nonstop questions, we reached the summit of our hike. From our vantage point we had a 180-degree vista that showcased the beauty of the mountains and the valley below. As the boys lingered on the mountain, I began to gently shift the topic from how I had become successful to questions that were designed to excavate their hearts. I thanked the Holy Spirit for this shift in strategy and asked, "What draws you both to success?"

There was a short silence as the boys searched for an answer to my unusual question. Their responses were similar. "We want to build something that matters."

The first young man added, "I work for a company with tens of thousands of employees. All I do all day is update presentations and spreadsheets. I guess I just want to believe that what I'm doing makes a difference." He paused for a moment, before adding, "I also want to call my own shots."

"It's good to be mission-driven," I replied. "That helped me tremendously on my entrepreneurial journey. But there's an entirely different set of challenges that comes when you own a business—and you'll always have some type of a boss, whether it's your customers, your business partner, or your shareholders." I smiled and the boys nodded back. "And remember, especially in the beginning, you're in charge of *everything*—payroll, growth, regulatory issues, compliance. The list goes on! Being the owner is fraught with responsibilities and risks."

I paused to see if these boys were open to this shift in our conversation and willing to explore a different and deeper way of thinking. The Holy Spirit was showing me how to relate to these boys and then gave me the right words to shift the conversation. I continued with passion and excitement. "But there's something much more important to consider. When I was your age, I was ambitious and climbed the corporate ladder faster than anyone else I knew. Once I landed my first leadership position, I realized I'd climbed so quickly that I'd failed to build a firm foundation. I'd 'arrived,' as they say, but it felt like being at the top of a flagpole as gusts of wind tossed from one side to the other."

I paused again to make sure they were still with me. "Today everyone talks about how to be successful, but almost no one talks about the importance of building your character. If I could distill everything I've learned over the last twenty years into a single sentence, it would be this: Who you become is much more important than what you achieve."

> **Who you become is more important than what you achieve.**

I could see the light bulbs going off as they absorbed my hard-earned wisdom. As my words washed over them, I stood amazed at how the Holy Spirit turned a superficial conversation about success into an eternal conversation about our identity. I also heard my own words with more clarity. In an instant, the journey that I'd been on for so many years was simplified down to that simple sentence. A sentence that I'd share with two strangers in the middle of a mountain range in a chance encounter. I had longed so deeply for Jesus to meet me in power and wonder on the mountaintop. I had thought that the only way to do it was in complete silence. And yet it was in the disruption of my plans and speaking with the boys that Jesus spoke to me in the most unexpected way.

We spent another hour talking at the summit. It was exhilarating to both encourage these boys who were at the start of their career and give them the advice I wish someone would have given me in my early twenties. By 2:00 p.m., the boys realized that if they stayed much longer at the summit, they might miss the last bus down the mountain. We said our goodbyes, and I gave them the two business cards I had thrown in my bag just moments before zipping it up.

As they headed back down to the mountain, I sat down on a log that overlooked the range and realized that for the next twelve hours, I had the mountain all to myself. As the silence of nature washed over me, I sat in awe of the day and the extraordinary world around me. Pulling a copy of the book of Ephesians out of my backpack, I began to read Paul's words out loud from atop the mountain. With over five hours until sunset, I was able to let the cares of the world slip away as I spoke my God's Word back to him atop a mountain He created. The slowness of reading a few verses and pausing to pray for their application in my life and the life of others had a cathartic effect. Eventually, I got to Ephesians 3:20–21, which captured the essence of this journey and the hope we all have in Jesus. "Now to him who is able to do immeasurably more than all we ask or imagine, according to his power that is at work within us, to him be glory in the church and in Christ Jesus throughout all generations, for ever and ever! Amen."

Sitting in the wilderness surrounded by the sounds, smells, and beauty of the landscape, I reflected on just how much my God had faithfully brought me through. In that moment, the worries of this season faded away and a smile crept across my face. The seeds of faith I had been planting all this time had finally found good soil. At first, I'd been impatient, expecting immediate results. Over time, I'd realized that both the sun and the storms of life had to do their work. The results that I longed for would come in time. Though the results lingered, I was finding the strength to wait. In doing so, I was living out Habakkuk 2:23, which says: "For the revelation awaits an appointed time; it speaks of the end and will not prove false. Though it linger, wait for it; it will certainly come and will not delay." I was finding that each journey through the valley gave me a little bit more strength, wisdom, and perseverance.

Chapter 21

FINDING PEACE

Just two days later, I was back at home acclimating to the challenges of a full schedule. This time, the chaos didn't catch me by surprise. I could see my growth and our family's growth so clearly. Joshua was making good progress. We were beginning to work as a united parenting team and creating a consistent environment for the kids. More importantly, we were starting to see our marriage as a sacred covenant worth fighting and sacrificing for. With each passing week, we were becoming better at looking past the issues on the surface and looking deeper toward each other's heart.

Joshua was now nine years old and while he had both good and bad days, he had matured enough to have deeper conversations with me. After a particularly frustrating day, I told him about my childhood learning disability and how Jesus had turned one of my greatest weaknesses, which was talking and communicating with others, into one of my greatest strengths. I explained how it had taken me years to realize this. I paused before relating this life lesson to him. "You have such big emotions, Joshua. You're learning to acknowledge and process them decades before I started to." I leaned in before sharing with him the truth I was trying to get into the depth of his heart. "Try not to worry, Joshua, our God is faithful. As it says in Jeremiah 29:11, He is able to make even the worst things work out for your good."

"Yeah, I know, dad," Joshua replied quietly, wiping tears from his eyes. He gave me one final hug before turning around to go find his brother and sister.

As a family, there was nothing especially different about this latest season of our lives, yet everything was different. The ups and downs and uncertainties were all still there, but Caitlin and I were different, and this was having a positive impact on our family. We were calmer, more grateful, and less stressed. For me, the challenges that once felt like tidal waves that crushed my heart were now more like ripples on a pond. I was finally able to take to heart the words of Jesus that he spoke in Matthew 6:34: "Therefore do not worry about tomorrow, for tomorrow will worry about itself. Each day has enough trouble of its own." Today, my cup overflowed and that was enough.

Joshua's Cub Scout campout was just a few weeks away and as our pack's committee chair, I was responsible for the logistics and planning. With about fifty campers expected, there was a ton of work to be done. By the time the weekend for the campout arrived, we were completely prepared. I had confirmed our reservations, recruited plenty of adults to help throughout the weekend, and picked up all the food for the campout. Our house looked like it was ready to feed a small army with boxes of food stacked all around the house.

On Saturday morning I woke up early and began the long process of loading all the food and our camping gear into the car.

As I began to take my second trip out to the car, Joshua walked up to me, sobbing. "Dad. It's not fair that this campout is all on you. You're working so hard and no one is helping."

"Oh buddy, it's okay!" I said, pulling him close to me and hugging him tight. "I like helping, and there will be lots of people to help once we get to the campsite."

"But it's not fair," Joshua protested.

I leaned back a little and looked Joshua in the eyes. "My precious boy, we are blessed to be a blessing. I do this because I love you and want other families to experience the joy of being together outside. Do you want to help me?"

Wiping away his tears, Joshua nodded and finished helping me load the car.

By eight thirty in the morning, we had arrived at the campsite and checked in. Joshua continued to help, and I marveled at just how far he'd come. At last year's campout, he barely had the attention span to help get our gear out of the car. Today, he had help set up our entire tent and hammered every single stake into the ground. Then he helped prepare all the picnic tables for lunch. He even made his way behind the food-serving station to stand with all the adults as he served every single kid and adult in the line.

"Buddy!" I said, walking over to him after lunch. "I can't believe you just served our entire Cub Scout pack! What made you want to do that?"

"I just wanted to help out, dad," he replied with an earnest smile.

I was grinning ear to ear. "Thank you so much! You must be so proud of yourself." As I watched my son walk off to be with one of his friends, I thought, *My son's deep feelings earlier this morning gave him the fuel to serve others.* Tears began welling up in my eyes. *Jesus, You are turning Joshua's weaknesses into strengths. Thank you!*

A few minutes later, one of the grandparents, a former scout leader, pulled me aside. "David, I have been so impressed with Joshua on this trip. Normally he's running around screaming like a banshee, but today he has been so courteous, so kind, so helpful. It's amazing to see."

> We serve a God who turns our weakness into strength.

I smiled and thanked him for his kind words. I knew Joshua would continue to have both mountaintop days like this and days that looked like we were heading in reverse. But I was no longer worried about the inevitable valleys that he would face. It had been a battle, but my son now knew I was there for him with complete and unconditional love—the type of love our Father in Heaven shows all of us. I thanked Jesus for what felt like a major turning point in both Joshua's life and mine. With the shouts of laughter and joyous kids running around, I whispered another quick prayer. "Jesus, thank You for today. Please help us to become the men You made us to be—to honor You in our daily lives."

Just a few weeks after our amazing camping trip in April 2025, Caitlin was putting breakfast on the table and Joshua began repeating something inappropriate that he'd heard someone at school say. Within moments, his brother was repeating it. Before I could even open my mouth, Caitlin whispered to me with a faint smile, "Don't even say a word."

"Okay," I whispered back. I walked over to Caitlin and said, "We'll definitely need to find some more time this summer to continue this conversation with the kids."

She smiled and said, "I know. They're growing up so fast."

A few moments later, the boys went back to their playful banter. In that simple moment, I saw what we had been fighting for all these years as parents—unity. This dream of two becoming one. An unnecessary crisis was averted as my wife led us beautifully through the moment. As a couple, Caitlin and I are still rebuilding the trust that was lost—and as parents, we still face daily ups and downs. But we've traversed enough distance of life's valleys to understand that we are never alone. God's faithfulness is ever present, and we have become okay even when everything is not okay. This is the essence of faith.

Now, almost three years into leaving my executive role at GreenWave, the days are different. I'm no longer racing to join 8 a.m. conference calls. Instead, I'm unloading

> **God's great promise is not that life will be perfect, but that we can have His peace, even in the trials.**

the dishwasher as the kids eat their breakfast. I've traded reviewing large strategic partnership agreements for double-checking division equations on homework assignments. And for the first time in my life, I see the heart of my family clearly: I see Joshua's tenderness, Ezra's passion for worshipping the Lord, little Ruth's fearlessness, and Caitlin's deep desire for our children to have beautiful memories from their childhood.

Somehow in this valley of pain and suffering, Jesus took each broken piece and created the most beautiful sculpture. It is not the opulent life of a senior executive that I had dreamed of as a kid. It is, instead, something that is so much more than I ever could have dreamed of or imagined. It is a life of fullness, where Band-Aids are used like stickers and neon markers find their way onto the canvas of our walls, furniture, and car interiors. Amid the battles to complete homework, the fights among the kids for what's theirs, and the hours in the day that never feel like enough, there is a grace and love that lingers deep in my heart. As we have learned how to stand in the tension, I have caught a glimpse of God's dream for family. A place with enough space for disappointment, big emotions, broken dishes, and lost spoons. A place of refuge where we don't have to worry about mistakes because we serve a God that works all things out for our good.

It took longer than I would have liked, but I'm no longer afraid of the valley. I have realized that each time I come out of the valley and reach a new summit, I leave a bit of my old self behind and become a little bit more like Jesus. When I am once again asked to trust the Lord our God and journey through yet another valley, I do so with just a bit more faith, hope, and love. It's a beautiful and sacred rhythm that is designed to build us up. This is the hope of our faith—that one day, as a result of walking through these valleys, we will be fully prepared to see our Savior with unveiled faces. It is this deep hope within us that John writes about in Revelation 21:1–5:

> I heard a loud voice from the throne saying, "Behold, God's dwelling is with the human race. He will dwell with them, and they will be his people and God himself will always be with them as their God. He will wipe every tear from their eyes, and there shall be no more death or mourning, wailing or pain, for the old order has passed away."
>
> The one who sat on the throne said, "Behold, I make all things new." Then he said, "Write this down, for these words are trustworthy and true."

I leave you with this simple message: Do not fear the valleys, for it is in these holy seasons of our lives that we wrestle with the broken places in our hearts and become more like Jesus. Even in the silence, the Lord your God is with you. His words are trustworthy and true, even in the valleys.

ACKNOWLEDGEMENTS

To Caitlin: Your grit, determination, and perseverance have shaped me into the man I am today. Your heart for our children has softened my rough edges and brought out love amid the chaos that I wouldn't trade for anything. You've challenged me to bring the best of us to our children each day. I am amazed at who they are becoming and how we get a front row seat to watch them unfold like brilliant flowers. Thank you for never giving up on us in the many valleys we have traversed.

To Kathy Meis: I never could have imagined that a happenstance meeting at a convention would, years later, lead to a published book. At every point in the process, you challenged me to dig deeper and connect the story more clearly for the reader. Without the tireless commitment and dedication from you and your team at Bublish, this book would be at best a shadow of what it is today. Words cannot express my gratitude for the countless hours you have poured in to make this book the best it could be. It has been a privilege to work with you and your team.

AUTHOR BIO

David Brenner was the first employee at a startup that grew to become a publicly traded company with a $1B+ market cap. As chief commercial officer, David played an integral role in building global strategic partnerships and raising capital for the company. After stepping away from the fast-paced startup world, he co-founded his own consulting firm with his father to help early-stage companies grow with purpose.

Married since 2013, David and his wife are raising their three children alongside their two dogs, Nala and Biscuit. When he's not working or with family, David finds renewal in nature, most recently on a solo backpacking trip in Zion National Park. Journey Through the Valley is his literary debut, offering a powerful reflection on perseverance, purpose, and spiritual growth.

www.ingramcontent.com/pod-product-compliance
Lightning Source LLC
LaVergne TN
LVHW011828060526
838200LV00053B/3936